TUNING THE

SYMPHONY

Space Wizard Science Fantasy
Raleigh, North Carolina

First Printing: 2016

Cover and interior art by Micah Epstein
Cover design and layout by Cheryl Perez

Library of Congress Control Number: 2016902451
ISBN 13: 978-0-9972994-0-3
ISBN 10: 0-9972994-0-3

Visit the author's website at williamctracy.com

For Mom:

Who always stopped reading to me just before the exciting part, so I would come back for more the next day.

TUNING THE

SYMPHONY

By

William C Tracy

MAJUS

- Maji have a long tradition of training suitable apprentices and, after many years of dedication, testing them in pairs to determine the better candidate. There is no rule saying one who can change the Grand Symphony must belong to the maji, but where else would they go? The maji control passage between the ten homeworlds, regulate disputes, and give aid during natural disasters. It is an honor to belong to their order.

From "The Houses of the Maji," by Ribothari Tan, Knower, later of the Council of the Maji

Rilan Ayama stood at the great crystal wall. It stretched both left and right, taking up the entire fourth side of the testing room, like a tremendous shop window. She was in the largest single chamber in the Spire of the Maji, occupying nearly the entire twenty-first floor, but the room on the other side of the wall was even larger.

Hesitantly, she placed one hand against the cool surface. On the other side, the six councilmembers stood, waiting on the wood floor constructed inside the hollow crystal column adjacent to the Spire. They were the highest ranking maji among the ten species. And they would all be testing her today. Her and Vethis. Only one would come out a full majus after today. The other would wait until the next quarter, though with another apprentice as a challenger. Rilan had heard of poorly testing apprentices waiting for three or four cycles while others were raised in favor of them.

She looked down at the crumpled piece of paper in her other hand. The note had been terse, unsigned, but she knew it was from Origon. How could the man write such a cryptic note, when he talked so much?

Just received news of family matter. May be late. Come see me after. Important decision to discuss.

As if she was raised to majus already, when she still had to test.

She was alone in the testing room, for now. Vethis was late as usual. The audience would file in later, including her and Vethis' mentors. It was a tradition. In a society of ten alien species, coexisting in the Nether—the common place to which all ten homeworlds connected—traditions were important.

Rilan had read the note over and over since a panting apprentice delivered it to her while she climbed to the testing floor, but hadn't been able to untangle any new information. She shook her head and stuffed the paper back into the pouch at her belt. Origon had promised to watch her test. She hoped he wouldn't be too late. Her insides were twisted in nervous knots quite enough. Vethis was lazy and narcissistic, but he had areas where he outshone her, if she was being honest.

Zsaana, the old councilmember for the House of Healing, her house, beckoned with a gloved claw. It was a perfunctory gesture for her to enter the immense crystal column standing adjacent to the Spire of the Maji, like a tree supporting a slumped bear. Many rooms of the Spire opened to the column. But the column vanished out of sight in the distance above. The Spire was merely forty-two stories tall.

Rilan took a deep breath and pushed her hand gently against the crystal surface, dark flesh against unbreakable material, willing it to give way. She had only passed twice before into one of the columns, big around as buildings, that supported the expanse of the Nether. It was a thing only maji could do, ensuring they were the only ones present inside the column at an apprentice's testing. She listened for the Grand Symphony of the universe, or that portion she could hear. It came after the briefest moment, a single high vibrato string that split into an entire orchestra, and then an orchestra of orchestras. Most of the notes rushed past far faster than she could comprehend. It was the music that underlay the universe. Change one chord, one note of the Symphony, and the universe changed with it.

She let the sound fill her, listening to individual notes and phrases in the melody of the House of Healing. She heard music defining her breath and movement, her skin, and her thoughts. Her senses extended to everything biological within range, from the shifting rhythms and accelerandos of the

Councilors, to the brisk notes describing insects living in the wood and stone walls of the Spire. She heard her own song—that composition which both defined her existence and let her change the Grand Symphony of the universe—blend with the column as her hand sank into the crystal surface. Harder than diamond, yet yielding to her, she heard snatches of music making up the essence of the Nether itself. It was, in some part, also a biological entity. No one knew where it came from, or even where it was located, in relation to the ten homeworlds, but it was where the early maji met others of their kind and began relations between the different alien races. Now it was the heart of the Great Assembly of Species.

She pushed into the outer wall of the column, its material parting before her. Colors sprang into existence, running along invisible paths. Emerald green for the House of Strength. Diamond yellow for the House of Communication. Blazing orange for the House of Power. Cool blue for the House of Grace. Pure white for the House of Healing—her house. And finally Rusty brown for the House of Potential. The column wall was several strides thick and she passed through as if walking through thick syrup.

As Rilan emerged into the open interior column, she sucked in air, though she hadn't felt the need within the wall. A smell of old wood and stale air tickled her nose as she stepped onto the floor built inside the column. It was high above the ground, but there were other floors in the column, above and below, each with its own specific purpose, connecting to a floor in the Spire of the Maji. The bottom of the floor above her was several stories overhead.

The councilmembers were arrayed in a line twenty strides away, and she crossed the distance to them, wiping sweaty palms against her dark leather pants. It was a pair her father made for her by hand. Her dark hair fanned out down her back and she swept a hand along it, trying to coax it to lie in a single bunch. She really should have tied it, but hated the feeling of it all bound up.

Speaker Karendi, head of the House of Communication and de-facto voice for the Council, stepped forward. The Kirian's garish robe flowed across bare knees, her crest of feathery hair flaring to show her welcome.

"I am believing there should be two apprentices testing this day, not just...ah."

Rilan looked over her shoulder to see Fernand Vethis pushing through the wall of the column, looking for a moment like a man suspended in ice. Once through, he tugged at his sleeves, straightening the blue-black crushed velvet coat. He was dressed as if he had just come from a party in High Imperium, with striped pants, white cuffs and cravat. It was a wholly unpractical thing to wear to a test designed to mentally and physically wear out the participant. But fitting, for him.

Vethis grinned as if he had already been chosen to become a majus today. They had been rivals since the first time they met as apprentices. Vethis was from a wealthy family, she from a poor one. He believed the maji were better than everyone. She just wanted to serve the Great Assembly. He was a social-climbing, toadying, power monger. The only reason he hadn't tested before now was he was unforgivably lazy, and preferred to cheat off his peers. He was everything that could be wrong with a majus.

Rilan showed her teeth in what could be construed as a smile by someone who didn't know her. As Vethis came abreast of them, smoothing back his long and oily black hair, Speaker Karendi continued.

"Only one of you will be leaving this chamber as a majus. Apprentice Ayama, Apprentice Vethis, it has been a pleasure for us to be devising these challenges specifically for each of you. Remember, there is always a way to pass each test, even though you are to be pitted against councilmembers." The Kirian's speech was less convoluted than most of her species, trained by cycles of acting as the Council's Speaker to the Great Assembly of Species.

"If you both will be stepping this way, Councilor Huar will be testing Apprentice Ayama first, against the House of Strength. On the other side of the column, Councilor Feldo will be testing Apprentice Vethis, against the House of Potential. The rest of us shall be observing, from a safe distance, of course." Speaker Karendi flashed her pointed teeth, her feathery hair rippling in what the Nether interpreted as anticipation. The Nether's translation of social gestures and language fostered cooperation and understanding, for the most part, keeping all ten species in relative peace.

Rilan drew in a shaky breath. The councilors made the tests unique to each aspiring apprentice, so she and Vethis would not have the same challenges. She didn't want hers to be easy, of course, but she also wanted to pass and become a full majus. Vethis gave her a self-satisfied smirk.

"May the best man win," he told her. Rilan stared back. She hated his clipped, affected accent.

"Or woman." Maybe she wouldn't mind if her tests were easier than his. She turned away. Better to concentrate on her own evaluation. Put the irritating man out of her mind.

Rilan found the head of the House of Strength and bowed. Councilor Huar bowed back slightly, then smiled, teeth open and tongue out. The massive Festuour was dressed in only a bandolier of pockets across her furry green-brown chest, a pair of glasses perched on her long snout in front of bright blue eyes, and a massive floppy pink hat sitting astride her ears.

"Come on girl. We have a match. I wanted to get yours in special, before I retire."

Huar led Rilan to a large table with two chairs, set near the far wall of the hollow column. Across its diameter, larger than most buildings, Rilan saw the other councilors watching, each at their own post. Vethis was chatting comfortably at Councilor Feldo, who seemed to be frowning back. Behind them, she could see foggy glimpses of the Imperium city, capital of the Nether, outside the translucent walls opposite the Spire of the Maji. She chewed her lower lip, heart hammering against her ribs.

"Now, I suppose we should do this formal-like." The Festuour settled her girth in the chair on the far side of the table, behind a collection of tiny pots and vines. "Sit, sit. Don't stand there gawking."

Rilan sat on a wooden chair opposite the councilor, somewhat heavily. She wrinkled her nose at the smell of dirt and decay. On her side of the table was a collection of vermin, tiny furry or scaled jaws gaping in death, collected from alleys of Imperium city. There were ten of them, each fitted with a small humming talisman.

The councilor touched a button on the side of the board and the little vermin started to twitch, crawling spastically forward. Rilan started at the sudden animation. "I, Councilor Jasrimopobt Huar, Grower, head of the House of Strength, challenge you to overcome my test and show yourself worthy of the House of Healing. Break my defenses."

Councilor Huar gestured three-fingered hands, her ears cocking forward, sliding across her pink hat's brim. An emerald green aura enveloped her as she changed notes in that part of the Grand Symphony she could hear. Rilan knew the House of Strength dealt with physical strength, of course, but also constitution, growth, and sustenance. It also dealt with living beings, overlapping somewhat with musical phrases from Rilan's house.

The plants in front of the councilor perked up as she adjusted the Symphony. A vine stretched forward and snapped at a crawling lizard that spasmed in range, throwing it back to Rilan's side of the table. She narrowed her eyes at the board, nervousness fleeing.

As vines reached forward, grabbed a furry scrounger, and tore it in half, Rilan opened herself to the Symphony. Fractal orchestras tumbled through her mind and she waded through the musical phrases. Some were too fast for her to understand before the tune played out. Her skill lay more in the mental side than the physical. She was training to become a psychologist, not a medical doctor, as Vethis was.

There was a complex musical phrase controlling the dead things. Since she could hear it, it must be of the House of Healing. Rilan guessed it had been stored by a majus of the House of Potential in the talismans attached to the creatures' backs. Otherwise, the music would have faded away by now.

A large flower scooped down, holding another lizard hostage. Down two creatures. Rilan found the melody defining musculature and bone density, taking a moment to understand the tempo and rhythm. Without doing so, a majus might fail to effect a change correctly. She inserted notes taken from her own song into the Symphony, increasing the tempo, making notes forte that were previously piano, increasing their intensity. The white glow of the House of Healing encircling her fingers as the creatures crawled faster, dodging the snapping vines. Rilan spared a glance to see Councilor Huar's large tongue caught between her fleshy lips. The plants sped up in response.

Rilan would not be able to make the same change twice in the same way, but neither could the councilor. The universe resisted changes to the Symphony, and if a majus tried to repeat the same change either before enough time had passed or while too close to the original change, it would fail.

Instead, she flexed her fingers like she was grabbing something, and caught the music defining the creatures' skin, using her song to change it. The white aura around her fingers was joined by her secondary color, only just starting to appear. The colors, indicative of the house, were only visible to a majus. Flecks of dull olive green sparkled in the white aura. The lizard-like creatures shuddered, scales growing and toughening to protect against vines and sticky flowers. Huar's green of the House of Strength began to show her own secondary color, the hue of peach flesh, as she put forth more effort. Each majus had a secondary color, and as the majus grew in experience, the unique color grew bolder, like a magical personality.

The vines thickened in response. Rilan grew sharper teeth on her rodents. The flowers reactions became more efficient.

Another lizard was plucked away and thrown off the table.

Evolve, defend, repeat.

Rilan adjusted the vermin's response to her commands, but they were thrown back again.

Her mentor told her never to go against the House of Strength head-on, and now she believed him. She couldn't win that way. But she threw six of her seven remaining creatures into a desperate rush, straight toward the plants.

Huar watched them so intently Rilan saw her miss the seventh creature, a little furry thing, scamper under the side of the table. She worked furiously to change the melody, rearranging internal organs, making room for chemicals to mix in ratios a body should never have.

As the vines and flowers pushed her vermin back, the little furry saboteur crawled over the far side of the table, behind Huar's line of plants. Its body shifted, muscles squirming under flesh. It stopped behind the center of the councilor's defense, and with a tiny squeak, exploded.

Rilan's other creatures rushed through the hole of burnt plant fiber.

Councilor Huar sat back with a puff of air. Rilan reversed the changes she had made to the Symphony, feeling her song flow back to her, and the rest of the vermin began drifting aimlessly, back to their original condition. Each person had their own song, and each song only had so many notes. Maji were careful to make changes that could be reversed. If a majus instead made permanent changes to the music, notes of their song would be lost until they slowly grew back, based on individual experiences. Until then, the majus would be less able to effect complex changes, their song no longer whole.

"Mighty fine," the councilor said. She swept her massive hat off and dabbed at the fur underneath, patting it back into place. "That's me beaten, fair. Go on now, see what the speaker has in store for you."

Rilan stood up shakily and nodded to the councilor. She glanced past to see the light outside the column was darker than before. Vethis was already with the head of their house, Councilor Zsaana. The two were bent over a table, and though she could see flashes of white light, they were too far away for her to hear the changes in the Symphony. What mattered was that he was ahead of her. Did that mean he had done better?

She walked toward Speaker Karendi where she stood at a podium, slowing her steps to sneak a look into the Spire of the Maji. The room on the other side of the column wall was starting to fill up with maji and other apprentices. She didn't see Origon, and made an effort to relax her shoulders.

Come on, Origon, you've been waiting for this test as much as I have. His tardiness was not helping her stress level.

The head of the Council coughed to get her attention, and Rilan looked away from the crystal wall. "I am to be the Speaker Mareveluchi Karendi, head of the House of Communication. I am challenging you to defeat my test and show yourself as being worthy of the House of Healing.

Overcome my speech." She stepped behind the podium, looming over Rilan. It hid her bright robe, pink and brown with yellow accents. The Kirians, of which the speaker and Origon were both members, were known for their garish dress.

Rilan felt a knot of worry forming in her stomach. Kirians were also famous for their public speaking and discourses on philosophy.

"Why are you here?"

"Um." Rilan adjusted to the new test as she looked into the speaker's gray eyes and pointy smile. "To become a majus."

"Why?"

Rilan swallowed. Her throat was constricted. A subtle yellow light, flecked with dark brown specks, surrounded the speaker. Yellow for the House of Communication, brown for the majus' personal color. "I want to use my ability to help…people." She had to swallow in between words. How was this a test of her house? "I'm going to become a psychologist." Was it a mental challenge of some sort? That was her strength, and Speaker Karendi knew it.

"Do you think the House of Healing is needing one of your abilities? Why are you unique? Would not Apprentice Vethis be a better choice?"

Rilan fought to push words out. It was getting hotter and the air felt like molasses. "I'm the…best in my class…I can change the Symphony…in ways they can only imagine…" She sagged. It was a strain merely to speak. She could barely draw breath and her vision was fogging. The speaker was doing something to the Symphony of the air, the medium of communication, changing its density or—

"Are you so arrogant to think you are being better than maji who have studied longer than you have been alive?"

The words had a force behind them, driving into her brain. What was she worth, really? Speaker Karendi was affecting her, persuading her. A two pronged attack. She struggled to hear the Symphony.

"Why are you able to hear the music when there are so many who cannot do this?"

She *could* hear the Symphony. She had since she was a child. Focus.

"I can...hear the Symphony...because I am unique...I—" Her words choked off and Rilan diverted effort into listening. There it was, very faint, the cloud of impulses that was Speaker Karendi. Chords flashed by, almost too quick to hear.

"If you are being so unique, give me the correct answer to this question. You are Speaker for the Council. Your species has gone to war against the Lobath, but you know they are in the wrong. How do you advise the Great Assembly?"

Rilan shook her head. She thought furiously over the answer while she put her notes of her song into in a Symphony the speaker couldn't hear.

"I must stay neutral in my answer, not favoring either side."

Pheromones were the answer, subtly influencing. She could do pheromones.

"You did not answer the question. Give me a definite solution."

The speaker pounded her with unsolvable dilemmas, unfair rulings, and tempting but unethical situations. Rilan devoted as much of her mental attention as she dared to the questions, answering as best as she could, gasping through the alternating thin and thick atmosphere. With the other part of her attention, she changed notes. Attraction. Distrust. Fight. Flight. Fear. Confusion. The notes were familiar to her. She had worked with many other apprentices, practicing her skill at mental healing.

"A Sathssn has been caught killing another of her species…" Speaker Karendi shook her head. "…But there is evidence that points to…" She raised a liverspotted hand to her head, smoothing back the crest of feathery hair that popped up in sudden apprehension. Rilan took a quick step forward, closing the distance between them. She touched the speaker, and a new Symphony exploded in her head, the kind that was only available in very close quarters. Rilan changed the speaker's mind.

Karendi's stern demeanor fell away at once and the pressure against Rilan's vocal chords ceased.

"I find I am unable to be competitive against you." She smiled pointily. Rilan had momentarily blocked her sense of ambition, simply a matter of changing notes defining the way the brain's receptors fired. "Well done." The smile faltered. "I am assuming this will dissipate soon?"

"In a few moments, Speaker," Rilan said. She began disassembling the changes she had made, regaining the phrases of her song. That little bit that was not reversible would replenish with a good night's sleep.

"Then you will be testing against the House of Power. I believe I will be checking with Councilor Zsaana just in case, to make sure there are no lasting effects."

Rilan bowed and moved on, walking around the perimeter of the column. Two down, four to go. She wondered if that was the way she had been supposed to complete the test. It had taken less time than the first. Vethis was just finishing his test with Zsaana. Had he done better than her? *Was* there a right way?

She looked to the other side of the column again. Had their whole class of apprentices showed? Certainly Vethis' gambling and drinking buddies were there. Were any there for her, or had they all come to cheer Vethis on? She had fewer friends than he, and fewer her own age. One in particular was still missing. Where was Origon?

Her next challenge was from the head of the House of Power, a corpulent Lobath who had occupied the post since before she was born. Though he was near sixty cycles old, he was still the craftiest on the Council. It was appropriate, as the

House of Power dealt with connections, relations, power structure, as well as heat and fire.

This time, she was to beat the house head at Hidden Chaturan, something specifically suited to the House of Power. One who could see the relations between things had a much easier time of determining where the pieces were hidden under the board.

Rilan struggled against the crafty Councilor while the light outside the column slowly died. Where was Vethis? Was he doing better than she? A quick glance around told her the oily man was finishing up with the councilor for the House of Grace. She was lagging behind. And on top of that, Origon was still not here.

The councilor moved another piece off Rilan's edge of the board. "That is not your test, apprentice, this is. Stop looking away."

Rilan pulled her gaze away from the wall, and back to the board. Of course the councilor would see that connection as well—her nervousness about Vethis and Origon. She tried to hold the whole board in her mind, but it was impossible, with the confounded rotating hatches hiding pieces.

Finally, she beat the Councilor, barely, and only by using the Symphony of Healing to follow the Lobath's movement impulses. He sat back with a groan, wiping a bead of sweat from between the base of his head-tentacles. "A rousing game, apprentice. If you are up for another game of Hidden Chaturan in the future, look me up. Now, off to the House of Grace."

Rilan stood, stretching, and took a few steps to wake up her legs. She had no idea how long she had been sitting at the little table, and turned to find Vethis in front of her. They were both standing near the center of the column.

"Finally done, Ayama? Took you long enough." Vethis adjusted his crushed velvet coat, though it looked in better order than her shirt, wrinkled from sitting at the table for so long. "I don't see that ratty old professor you hang around— the one no one likes?" Vethis made a show of looking around in surprise. "In fact, did anyone come here to see you besides your own mentor?"

Rilan resisted the urge to hit him. The best way to deal with Vethis was to ignore him. Anything else would only rile up the fop.

"At least I didn't have to pay my friends to attend." *So much for staying silent.*

"Aaahaha." Vethis gave his fake laugh to go with his affected accent. It was the way the richer echelons of High Imperium spoke. "Well, as they say, at least I can *afford* to have friends." He gave her a condescending smile. "Tests going well for you? Fortunately I got the harder part done first. Just need to coast through the rest. Watch out for Councilor Zsaana—I think the old snake has it in for those of his own House. He did some things with the House of Healing I'd never seen before."

Rilan thought of the way she passed the speaker's test, and how she barely scraped by against the House of Power. Surely

Vethis wouldn't do better than her, but then the tests were different for each apprentice.

"I'll do just fine," she told him. "After all, I studied for this."

"Yes, top marks in the class and all that. Of course, sleeping with your philosophy professor probably helped."

"I didn't—" Rilan clenched her fists. Vethis would take anything she said about Origon the wrong way. "At least my father didn't buy my grades for me."

"No, I don't believe he's ever seen that much money in his life." Vethis waved his hand as if to shoo her along, the lace at his wrist fluttering limply. "Can't stay to talk, I'm due to be raised a majus, after all." He headed to the table where the head of the House of Power still sat.

"You can't bribe the councilors," Rilan called after him. She *hoped* he couldn't bribe the councilors. She sighed.

Rilan glanced across the translucent column and saw the crowd in the connecting room in the Spire of the Maji. As she moved to the next station, the figures on the other side became clearer. Her eyes flicked over Farha Meyta, her mentor, and she frowned. Where was Origon? He should have been front and center at her test. He had been talking about her transition to full majus since her graduation from university. Surely news of his family could wait a little longer.

She pursed her lips and gathered her hair back with both hands. She was distracted, and in addition, Vethis had made her doubt herself. She knew it objectively, but that didn't actually help the queasy feeling in her stomach. Her psychology training wasn't helping her now.

She had to put all this out of her mind, or it would hinder her test. Either Origon would show or he wouldn't. And if he didn't, she prayed Vish would give him strength to heal quickly from what she would do to him.

The Etanela who was head of the House of Grace was immensely tall, even for one of her species. Rilan felt her back straighten as she strained for an extra finger's-breadth of height. The councilor bowed down to speak to Rilan, the bluish cast of her skin transitioning to the pale blue-blond mane of hair all around her head and long neck.

"Are you ready, apprentice?" she asked. Rilan nodded. They were at a roped obstacle course, dotted with little paper flags. The Etanela crouched down and smoothed her mane of hair, affixing it with a short length of string behind her neck. Her fingers tied a complex knot in the string with ease, fingers glowing slightly with the blue of her house.

Showoff.

Rilan crouched next to him, wondering what the signal would be to start. Would there be a—

A horn blared and the councilor was off, long legs taking steps five times hers. Rilan puffed after her. *Did Vethis have to do this? He couldn't have been so put together if he'd just ran a race.*

This was a test of the physical, how the efficiency of the House of Grace could compare against the body-changing aspects of the House of Healing. Just like the other tests, she would not win if she stayed on the defensive. Rilan reached mentally while she ran, trying to hear the chords defining the councilor's legs. They jangled and went in and out of hearing. She grabbed at the notes as she could, trying to slow the Etanela down. Physical changes from a distance with the House of Healing were not her specialty. She was better at the mental aspect. At least training with her father prepared her for the exertion. Breathe in through the nose, controlled pulse out through the mouth. Repeat.

The obstacle course was not easy, and she barely stayed abreast of the councilor, even with the changes she effected. The councilor flowed through the obstacles, meanwhile, she bumbled through, moments behind, looking like a horse swimming next to a dolphin.

When the end of the course came up, she tried to tally things in her head. Had she hit five flags or six? She was nearly certain the councilor had touched nine, all with her help. Otherwise the tall woman wouldn't have touched one.

Speaker Karendi was waiting at the exit to the race. Rilan bent forward, resting hands on knees to get her wind back. She took in long sweet breaths, then undid the changes she still held, regaining her song. The Etanela wasn't even breathing hard. Her long arms were clasped behind her back. Who knew the councilor had such a competitive streak, especially for one of her placid race? At least it had kept Rilan from thinking about who was—and was not—watching. She looked over to the table at the House of Power. Vethis was still bent over the board with the Lobath Councilor. Maybe she didn't do too badly.

"You were having a lag of six seconds, apprentice," Speaker Karendi said, "However, the Head of the House of *Grace*," she gave a sardonic pointy smile, "touched four more flags. I will be calling this test a tie. Your next challenger is Councilor Zsaana."

Rilan bowed to the two councilors, still panting a little, and straightened. Three wins and one tie, out of six houses. How had Vethis done? The final decision could go against her, even with all wins. A tie wasn't good. The next house was hers, but Vethis' warning flashed through her head. She had hoped for an easy win from the House of Healing.

She glanced to her growing audience. Still no Origon. This was more than just lateness, but she couldn't afford to think about him. After the test. Then she would find out what was going on. She tried to concentrate, but her stomach felt like it was twisting into knots.

Councilor Zsaana was standing in the middle of a circle painted on the floor, ten paces across. His face, as always, was hidden under his deep black cowl. Personally, she found his cat eyes and scaly skin unnerving, though the last time she had seen him without a hood was cycles ago. The shorter councilor stood with a hunch from age, gloved hands clasped behind his back, not a bit of skin showing. The only bright color on him was the small patch on the breast of his cloak, marked with the white of the House of Healing and the turquoise of his personal color.

As she stepped in the circle, his gravelly voice issued from the depths of his cowl: "I, Councilor Zsaana, head of the House of Healing, challenge you to overcome me. In this test, show yourself worthy of my house. Move me out of the ring."

He stepped back, front heel lifting, toe of his boot just touching. One gloved hand came forward, raised, palm up in front of his chest. The other now pointed down, warding off a blow. Rilan recognized the stance from the art called *Dancing Step* and automatically moved into the form of *Fading Hands*, the art she studied, her hands ready to catch or twist.

After the race? Really? Breathe in through the nose, out through the mouth. Conserve energy. Don't think about Origon. The familiar fighting form comforted and relaxed her. Maybe this wouldn't be so hard after all.

She moved forward in a straight line, but the councilor shifted off at an angle. This would not be a normal sparring match, not between two members of her house.

White and turquoise surrounded the councilor, but Rilan could hear the changes in the Symphony this time. Did those notes describe balance? Yes, and leg strength, she decided. The councilor was quick, shifting through measure after measure of the melody describing his body faster than she could even process the notes. He had cycles of experience over her. The speaker said the tests were made to be passed, but this was pure experience and skill. Rilan pushed the worry away—pushed all her worries away.

The councilor sprang, quicker than thought. One hand locked against hers, forcing it out while the other popped against her chest. She exhaled as she was pushed back, stopping just at the edge of the circle.

Rilan shook her head, adjusting her stance and then the Symphony, tightening musical phrases to freshen muscles tired from the race. It was a permanent use of notes from her song, and she would only be able to do it once, but it would give her more endurance for this fight. Losing that bit of her song was worth it. She stalked forward and the councilor moved back, keeping the distance between them the same. Rilan leapt.

Bone crunched against bone, hardened like steel.

The two circled, reassessing strengths and weaknesses.

The councilor's arm lengthened, muscles stretching past their normal limits to land a strike.

The straight lines of *Fading Hands* intersected the circular arc of *Dancing Step*.

Rilan caught a boot before it contacted her sternum, but only by increasing her reaction time.

Her hand moved a punch aside, twisting it so the councilor went backwards. But he snapped straight up, black cloak flapping, driving a punch that just brushed her nose as she pulled away from it.

Rilan staggered back, nose stinging and eyes watering. She sniffed back blood, then countered. Councilor Zsaana sidestepped it easily.

She was on the defensive again. This was her house, but she had to be better than its leader, who had forty cycles more experience. She scowled and ducked a backfist.

This wasn't a physical challenge. It was a mental one.

She studied the melody defining her opponent's mental state. This was her specialty, and she could understand more of the music from a distance than most. Add to that the closeness and understanding of sparring with someone, and she had a clear picture of what the councilor was thinking. They circled, trading blows that tested the other's defense.

He was calm, collected, and completely in charge of his situation. There was no place for her to start making changes without him noticing instantly. He'd either counter it or shrug it off.

She adjusted melodies in her body, the white and olive glow around her brightening. Councilor Zsaana's attacks increased, seeking every hole in her defense as he saw her rewriting the Symphony. She had to hope he was not as familiar with mental changes as physical ones.

Rilan's perceptions began to slow as she inserted the adjusted music made of her own song back into the Symphony. Zsaana's movement sped up to her eyes. She felt a rib creak as his gloved hand struck, palm forward. She was pushed back, but managed to recover, her thoughts fuzzy. Zsaana was moving like a projection at double speed and she backed up farther, desperately warding off strikes.

A booted toe touched a pressure point in her leg and she wavered to that side with a grunt. He circled and the next punch came at an oblique angle, just grazing his glove's leather against her chin. One of her teeth bit into her cheek.

She saw him gather for the last strike—the one that would push her backward out of the circle. Her mind was foggy now, and slow, like cold honey. There was something she had to remember, more important than anything else. It was a simple sequence of notes.

Oh yes.

She reversed what she had done, gaining the phrases of her song back.

As the councilor sprang forward, her mind cleared, her reactions increased, and she saw the opening she would not have before.

Councilor Zsaana struck, but Rilan spun to the side much faster than she had moved before, taking a stance from *Dancing Step*. She caught a flash of surprise in the cat's eyes deep under his hood as Zsaana flew past her, landing with the toe of one boot outside the circle.

Rilan turned to him and bowed. Councilor Zsaana gave a respectful tilt of his cowled head in return.

"Your technique, it has improved, but do not depend on such deception to save your life. It is risky. You are ready for your last test, apprentice."

Rilan walked to the only section of the testing area she hadn't yet visited, near where the Spire of the Maji met the wall of the column. Back across its width, Vethis was face to face with Speaker Karendi. She held on to the hope that he couldn't find a way to cheat his way through this test.

Outside, it was nearly full dark in the city. In the Spire of the Maji, she saw the crowd of onlookers craning to see her actions. Her eyes roamed the various maji and apprentices in vain.

Where is he?

She directed a raised eyebrow to Farha Meyta, but her mentor only shook his balding head. He didn't know either.

Rilan faced the last councilor.

The head of the House of Potential stared back impassively from under bushy black eyebrows, and Rilan finally looked away from the intense gaze. She had to stop thinking about Origon.

"This is the last one, apprentice," he cautioned, his voice resonant. "Keep your wits about you. You will need them."

Councilor Mandamon Feldo

Rilan glanced down at the worktable between them, holding a contraption made of interwoven gears, levers, and springs. Many separate pieces were clasped together, some with vials of fluids held between metal pistons.

"I, Councilor Mandamon Feldo, head of the House of Potential, challenge you to overcome my puzzle and show yourself worthy of the House of Healing. Disarm my bomb."

Her head jerked back up. Though he was the only councilor of her species, he was harder to read than some of the aliens.

"Time is wasting, apprentice."

Rilan focused on the contraption—the bomb—and swallowed. There were no biological pieces. There was nothing for her to affect with the Symphony. The parts were obviously artifacts made with the House of Potential, many with faint brown auras, storing energy and action in different combinations. They might also store effects from other houses. Each artifact could do something as sinister as suck the air from her lungs, or merely slip from her grasp. There was one way to tell, though she had rarely used that facet of the House of Healing.

Rilan dove into the Symphony, tracing the architecture of the convoluted thing with a finger, listening for the traces every person left in their wake. Far down in the melody there was a crumbling cadenza, the music deteriorated with age. But there was still evidence of fingers and breath touching it in the past, marking its construction. As she was only listening, and not changing, she would be able to do this multiple times. But the moment she used her song to change notes, the universe would close down on that potential for variation.

Rilan closed her eyes, listening to the story the notes told. There was a switch, carefully placed with bare fingers when arming the mechanism, just…there.

She pushed a point on a cubical piece, identical to every other part, and the pistons hissed, releasing the cube's grasp. She risked a glance up, to see Councilor Feldo's eyes trained on her, no expression on his face. His arms were crossed in front of his dark brown suitcoat.

"Do you imagine he'll arrive before you finish your test?"

Rilan frowned. "I have no idea." That wasn't fair. She bent back to her task, trying to focus on the notes. Her mind wandered to all the reasons Origon could be late. Of all the people not to be at her test. He was scattered when he chose to be, but whatever he was to her now; professor, friend…something more…she deserved more respect than this.

Origon, I'm going to kill you when this is over.

She became aware of the councilor's finger, tapping against his other arm, and shook her head, pushing the arrogant man from her mind.

The next part to the puzzle was more complex, having changed hands several times. Finally, she traced down the answer and pressed the correct combination of buttons on its side.

"I imagine even apprentice Vethis could finish this faster." Rilan tried to ignore the councilor's voice.

The next piece was shaped like a clenched hand, fingers closed into the palm. Bare skin had never touched it, and she darted an irritated look at the councilor. He stared back.

She dug even farther into the Symphony. This far down, chords and musical phrases sped by, faster than she could follow. Pieces were incomplete, like listening to one instrument playing something meant for a full orchestra.

She kept on, thoughts of Origon sliding into her concentration, disrupting her test.

So he isn't here. Why should that matter? Maybe he was only interested in a good student. Maybe I read his attentions wrong.

"Focus, apprentice. This is why inter-species relationships are frowned upon. Too much miscommunication."

What did the councilor know about it? Maybe he thought she should be with Vethis instead, just because he was near her own age and her same species? Rilan scowled up at him. Was that worry on his face? She snapped back to her task. Which piece was next?

There were several left, but this puzzle had many dead ends. She chose a clasp holding a box in its middle. It was the most likely to be her objective.

Something held the clasp closed, some infused air pressure captured by a member of the House of Communication. She looked into the Symphony to determine its source, peering past crumbling chords.

Origon had created it.

Her mind whirled, trying to understand. He had even contributed to her test. Why was he not here to see her succeed? Why wasn't—

Something inside the box began smoking.

Councilor Feldo reached out quickly, his hand ringed with the rust-brown color of the House of Potential. As he made contact with the box, the smoke died away, its energy transferred before it could explode.

The councilor flicked the air with a hand and a miniature firework shone sun-bright for a moment as the air heated incandescent, then faded.

"And that would be time, apprentice."

Rilan hung her head.

A few minutes later, she stood in the middle of the circular floor. To her right, lights were shining in the vast city outside the crystal column, especially in the High Imperium, where money and fashion were prevalent. The sons and daughters of senators, speakers, and other diplomats would be playing at cards, drinking wine, and dancing at balls. Vethis was beside her, seeming at ease, his velvet suit as unwrinkled as if he had just put it on.

To her left Farha Meyta still watched her eagerly from the Spire of the Maji, though some of the other spectators were playing card games or talking amongst themselves. Probably Vethis' friends who had grown bored of the tests. All six members of the Council of the Maji spoke amongst themselves in a little circle not far away, but no sound came to them.

"Concerned, Ayama?" Vethis asked. Only one of them would leave this column a full majus. The other would have to wait until the next rising apprentice from the House of Healing was ready.

"Of course not," she answered, though she felt as if she might be sick. Honestly, she was a good student. She shouldn't be worried. The tests were made to be passed. Otherwise she would have no chance to win against the senior maji who had become the heads of their respective houses. Yet she had tied one—barely—and lost another. She had no idea how well Vethis did. He could have been a good student if he applied himself instead of lazing about with his rich friends. It was one of the things about him that annoyed her most.

She looked up as rustling came to her. The councilors filed in a semicircle around her and Vethis, a vast difference in shapes and sizes, from the diminutive Councilor Zsaana to the towering Etanela councilor.

Speaker Karendi stepped forward just a little, used to being the voice of the Council. Her crest of feathery hair bristled, and the Nether translated it to an impression of someone settling a jacket. "We have been discussing your tests, apprentices. Your skills are not being in question. Both of you are having enough talent in the House of Healing to work with any of the other houses in our service of the Great Assembly."

Speaker Karendi looked at Vethis first. "Your natural skill in healing is impressive to several of the councilmembers." Vethis stood straighter at that, smiling.

The speaker turned to Rilan. "And with your talent for hearing and changing the Grand Symphony, you could rise far one day—maybe even to the heights of the Council."

Rilan felt a thrill rise through her. They thought she was that good? Then why were there frowns on some councilors' faces? She waited for the 'but.'

"But," Speaker Karendi continued, "the maji are servants of the ten species. We are creating the portals that connect the ten homeworlds with the Nether and with each other. Without us, there could be no Great Assembly of Species."

Her crest of feathery hair waved as if in a breeze. "Neither of you are yet willing to serve, to ignore distractions that take you away from your work. Apprentice Ayama, you go your own way, around the rules that hold our society together. You must be finding out what it means to be helping its inhabitants, instead. Apprentice Vethis, you are, bluntly, arrogant. You must learn to listen to those who know more than you. You would do well to study *with* Apprentice Ayama, and vice versa.

Each of you could teach the other something. Now, I will be giving over to my fellow councilors."

Rilan frowned at Vethis, and saw the same expression mirrored on his face. *That's never going to happen.* She looked back to the house heads.

Councilor Huar gave a big pink smile, tongue lolling in a Festuour smile. "You passed in my eyes, dear," she said to Rilan. "I'll be up for a rematch anytime." She turned to Vethis, not smiling so broadly. "You passed as well, though next time I wager you'll remember not to challenge the House of Strength head on." Rilan wondered what his test had been. It sounded like the Festuour favored her over Vethis.

Speaker Karendi's crest made a single flat line down the middle of her head. Decisive. "Apprentice Ayama, while your technique may be suspect—I am not enjoying being mentally adjusted—I must pass you on merit alone." She crossed bare liverspotted arms. "Apprentice Vethis, I am afraid you did not measure up to what I expected."

A straight win for her. Rilan felt a little bit of tension leave.

The councilor for the House of Power rubbed at his rubbery mouth with long fingers, watching Rilan. The tips of his three head-tentacles twitched around his shoulders. "Try not to keep the company of *that man* so much. Nothing good will come of such an inter-species dalliance."

Rilan felt her eyebrows climb. How widely known was their relationship? This was the Nether, not a backwards homeworld. Still, she caught a nod of agreement from some of the other councilors out of the corner of her eye. The Lobath councilor looked to his left and the next councilor. It seemed that was all he had to say. What did that mean? Did she pass or did Vethis? She caught her rival frowning as well.

The head of the House of Grace paused for a moment, looking upward from her great height. "A pass for both. There are not many who can rival me at the obstacle course. I am frankly surprised either of you came as close as you did."

Yep. Still an ass. And still no help to decide who would become majus. The twisting feeling in Rilan's stomach returned.

Councilor Zsaana folded gloved hands together, the opening of his hood pointing to Rilan. "Today, I am afraid I cannot pass you." She gaped, and some of the other councilors even looked surprised. "Your technique, it is good, but ineffective. In real combat, with intent to injure, your technique would be impractical and you would be quickly defeated. My vote, it is going to Apprentice Vethis." And after Vethis' report to her, she was sure she had that one locked down. What test had the councilor set for Vethis?

Councilor Feldo glared at her under his bushy eyebrows. His eyes flicked to Zsaana and back to her. "My vote was to fail you and pass Vethis. Before I do that, one question. Apprentice, why did you fail to defuse my bomb?"

Rilan opened her mouth, hesitated. Her first inclination was to say she should have used some better method, but she knew that was untrue. She could tell the way she answered this question would be important, maybe to her future as a majus.

"The truth, apprentice," Feldo warned.

Rilan forced the answer out, but kept her eyes on the floor. "My attachments…no…my *attachment* got the better of me."

"And this is how it will always be." Rilan looked up to Feldo in surprise, and saw Speaker Karendi frown. "Keep that in mind. A pass for Apprentice Ayama."

Rilan blinked.

Speaker Karendi looked her councilors over. "If I am understanding your votes correctly, both Apprentices have passed four of their tests and failed two. In everything, the Council must be unanimous. Which apprentice shall we pass? Please be giving your vote to one or the other."

In turn, each of the councilors gave their answer.

"The House of Strength passes Apprentice Ayama."

"The House of Communication is also passing Apprentice Ayama."

"The House of Power passes Apprentice Vethis."

The tall Etanela councilor hesitated, hands smoothing back her mane of hair. She had been one to pass both of them. Then, "The House of Grace passes Apprentice Vethis."

"The House of Healing passes Apprentice Vethis," Councilor Zsaana growled beneath his dark cowl.

"And the House of Potential passes Apprentice Ayama." Councilor Feldo crossed his arms. "I believe we are tied again, Councilors. Is someone willing to change their vote?"

Several hundred ages of the universe went by, and no one spoke. Rilan's stomach felt like lead, and she pressed her hands to her leather pants to keep them from shaking. She saw Vethis smoothing his coat again and again, though it was as straight as it was going to be.

Gradually, Rilan got the impression of eyes staring at her from under Councilor Zsaana's hood. "My vote, I will be willing to change. Pass for Apprentice Ayama."

Rilan sagged. She heard Vethis stamp a foot, and for once, couldn't blame him. He must be surprisingly competent when testing for them to be tied. He had never been a good student at university.

"Welcome, Majus Rilan Ayama, to the House of Healing," Speaker Karendi intoned. "Henceforth you will be granted all privileges of majus status, including rooms, stipend, and a seat in the Great Assembly. You will also be required to fulfill all duties, including operating portals to the various homeworlds in equal portion to other maji." The speaker let a smile show her pointy teeth. "Congratulations." She turned to Vethis. "Do not let this be disheartening you, apprentice. With such a close test, I am sure you will be making majus next time."

The others followed suit, congratulating her in their various manners, and offering condolences to Vethis. One by one they passed through the wall of the column back into the Spire of the Maji proper, to the applause and commiseration of the waiting crowd.

After that, it was all smiles, and handshakes, and back pats for Rilan. She spoke to all those who had watched from outside the column. Even some of Vethis' friends came over to congratulate her, seeming sincere.

Rilan returned every smile she got, even going so far as to shake hands with Vethis, though he did try to squeeze her knuckles off. Afterward he went to talk with his mentor, a small majus of the House of Healing who earned his living as a medical doctor.

Her own mentor, Farha Meyta, gave her a gift of a small white bell, imbued with a permanent investment of his own song and the Symphony of Healing, held to the bell by the craft of the House of Potential. He said it would ward off disease.

"It has been a pleasure, dear," he said.

"But now please get out of your apartment?"

Farha laughed good naturedly at her joke. "I'll admit, I am ready to be on my own again."

"Maybe you'll finally find a wife," she ribbed.

"Or another insufferable apprentice. I used to have hair before I took you on, you know." They clasped hands again. "Good luck, Rilan—Majus Ayama," he said. "I'm sure we will be seeing each other across the Great Assembly."

Rilan took her leave of her mentor—former mentor, and slowly started pressing toward the exit. She took one last look back at Vethis, who was now talking animatedly with a large Festuour she didn't recognize. He would become a majus eventually, and maybe this would inspire the lazy man to pay attention to his work, but she doubted it.

She headed for stairs down and out of the Spire of the Maji. Despite her forced calm, she was about to jump out of her own head. By Shiv's ponderous earlobes, where *was* that man?

ORIGON

- Inter-species relationships have been contentious since the species initially met in the Nether. From the first time an adventurous Methiemum flirted with an Etanela or a Festuour, these relationships have occurred. The xenophobic of the ten species deride such activities, though the majority are neutral. Few encourage such romantic ties even in the Nether, though it has more active long-lasting inter-species relationships than all ten homeworlds combined. On the worlds, a more conservative philosophy is the norm.

Excerpt from "A Dissertation on the Ten Species, Book I: Overview"

Rilan trudged up the spiral steps in the House of Communication, grumbling. Because of their connection with the air, some egotistical idiot many cycles in the past decided the physical House would be second in height to only the Spire itself. The House of Strength had it right, with half their headquarters at ground level, spread out in a vast circle. Even the House of Healing was only a few stories tall, connecting their members to the Imperium's medical research center.

But no, this had to be the tallest house and the arrogant ass that lived on the top floor was the one she was going to see. The climb only stoked her anger.

She paused for breath, leaning back on the carved balustrade dividing the top floor from a plunge to the ground floor far below. A hallway stretched out in front of her, wood and stone panels lit by lamps containing ever-glowing fires courtesy of the House of Power. The window at the end of the hall gave little light this late at night.

Rilan trudged down the hall, still muttering under her breath. If she wasn't so concerned over her former philosophy professor's absence at her testing, she might have just stewed at home.

She patted her pouch, with the note still in it. *No, I would have come anyway. At least be truthful to myself.*

Rilan knocked on Origon's door. Why he insisted on this particular apartment was beyond her. It was a waste of time just to run up and down the flights. She waited.

"Come on, Origon," she said to the door. There was a small card affixed in the middle with the majus' name, but aside from that, no decoration. "You have a lot of explaining to do, and I know you're at home." She was leaning into another knock when the door opened like a cork from a bottle.

Rilan nearly fell, but turned it into a stumble, right into his skinny arms. Origon looked terrible. His crest was drooping, feathery hair languid. There were circles under his large dark eyes, and his liverspotted Kirian skin looked more pale and wrinkled than usual. Even his feathery moustaches drooped, beneath the edge of his chin. The bright orange fabric of his robe only made him look worse.

Rilan resisted showing sympathy. "Why weren't you there? What was that note about?" She could see him pull himself together, pasting a false smile above the wisps of his feathery beard.

"I was knowing you would pass, wasn't I? No need to be there just to be distracting you." Origon paused. "You did pass, yes?"

"I very nearly didn't, thanks to you." She pushed at his chest and he stepped back, closing the door behind her with one foot. "You would have had to call Vethis majus, otherwise. Maybe I should take the councilors' advice and keep away from you." She saw the flash of irritation that crossed his face before he hid it. The Council and he were never on the best terms.

"Your father wasn't there either." He retreated as she stalked forward.

"My father is an indigent craftsman in the middle of the poorest city on Methiem. He flatly refused to 'embarrass' me by coming to the 'rich' Imperium, despite the fact I had special permission to create a portal directly to his house instead of using the portal ground. He's stubborn as a stone and I promised I would visit him as soon as I got my first vacation. What's your excuse?"

He was stalling. There was something else.

"I—" There was only a half second of pause before he answered, but she knew him well enough to catch it. "It is really not to be important—"

"Not buying it." Rilan kept moving forward, pushing Origon backward with the tip of one finger. He stumbled over a low yellow ottoman.

"The councilors were not wanting me there anyway—"

"I'll believe that, except maybe for Councilor Feldo." Thoughts of the artifact Origon contributed to flashed through her mind. "But when has the Council's displeasure *ever* kept you from doing exactly what you wanted?"

Origon's back hit the wall of his apartment and he sagged against it, face crumpling. Rilan's anger disappeared in a flash. Was that a tear?

"My brother…he is…I was just receiving the news before your test. I could not…"

She had never seen Origon so defenseless. She took the last step toward him and enfolded his larger frame. He buried his head in her shoulder.

Well, this wasn't how she expected to celebrate her graduation from apprentice to majus. She gently stroked the tiny gray feathers that made up the Kirian's hair. She loved the way pink and blue tufts fluttered in and out of sight as his crest responded to her touch. But his face was still buried against her best shirt.

"Want to tell me about it?" she ventured. She was, after all, the one training to be a psychologist. Although she didn't think her first real case would be comforting a man more than twenty cycles her senior, both her professor and her close friend.

Origon straightened, running a long finger along his cheek. She was always surprised he didn't poke himself in the eye with his claw-like fingernails. "I am sorry to be missing your testing, Rilan," he said, more contrite than she had ever heard. "Sit. I have something to ask."

She took a seat on the yellow couch, matching the ottoman he had tripped over. Origon sat beside her, straightening his garish robe's sleeves and length to cover ankles and wrists. It was a cultural thing for the Kirians, for the males to hide their legs and arms. She still didn't understand why, as the females showed so much skin. Origon had told her it wasn't anything religious. Just one of those customs that didn't translate well between species.

Origon picked up a little statue from a side table; a token from one of his many travels among the ten homeworlds. He idly fondled it, running fingers along the length. It was some animal she didn't recognize. His whole apartment was filled with knick-knacks, and as little time as he spent here, they were always covered with a layer of dust.

He didn't look at her as he spoke. "I will be having to leave tomorrow morning. It is another reason I could not be attending your testing." He waved a hand to where a small bag was half-full of clothes in a corner. "I must be discovering what happened."

"What did happen?" Rilan asked. She folded her hands in her lap. At least that explained the note. "What about your brother?"

Origon's face went through permutations of sadness, then straightened, becoming almost haughty. His hair slicked back to a neutral position. That was the man she knew.

"He is dead."

Origon didn't talk about his family much. Rilan knew he had the one brother, though both his parents had gone back to the Great Wheel of life and death before she met him.

"Oh. I'm so sorry," she said. She could only think how inconvenient a time it was for this to happen. She buried the thought.

It's a normal reaction to a message of grief. Stop focusing on yourself and help him.

"Will you be going back home to Kiria to handle his affairs?"

Origon, still fiddling with the carving, looked up at that. "No, I am going to Festuour."

"Festuour?" She had never been to the furry aliens' home world, though of all the homeworlds, it was the friendliest with her own. "What's there?"

"His body, so I am told."

Now she was confused. "He is not a majus, is he?"

"No. I am the only one of all my relations having that ability. And doubly fortunate in being able to hear the Symphony of two houses."

Rilan waved the fact away. Origon never grew tired of mentioning that he was a member of both the Houses of Communication *and* Power. "What business did he have on Festuour?"

"That I do not know." Origon's crest spiked and separated, the Nether translating it as confusion. "The communication was sent to me through a portal from a little city on Festuour being called Martflen."

"Never heard of it." But that wasn't very odd. She had only ever been on Methiem—her homeworld—and in the Nether, as it was the hub of communications between the homeworlds, and the headquarters of the maji.

"Nor I." That was stranger. Origon knew just about every nook and cranny of all ten homeworlds. His face showed pain for an instant, and Rilan knew his brother's death was eating at him far more than he would show. The emotions she saw when she arrived were likely the most she would get. It wasn't good for him to suppress that emotion, but he would never even admit he was doing it.

"Are you knowing what my brother did?" Rilan shook her head. "He was a lawman on Kiria—and very good at it. The last communication I was getting from him mentioned a far reaching case he had started, but gave no information except that someone had been killed."

"And Festuour?"

Origon shook his head, feathery hair flattening in negation. "That is something I will be discovering."

Rilan sighed. She had hoped they could spend more time together. "I'll let you get back to packing," she said, rising, then paused, searching his face. "When will I see you again?"

Origon's crest suddenly fluttered in agitation, and he put the little carving down, but continued to move his fingers restlessly. "That is to be the other part I wanted to talk with you about."

Rilan stood this time, turned to face him as he sat on the couch. "What is that?"

"Come with me tomorrow."

"To Festuour?"

"Yes." Origon leaned forward, pleading, his words coming out in a rush. "And after I am finishing this ancestor's cursed business with my brother, stay with me. Travel with me. We will be seeing all the homeworlds and their cultures, disagreements, religions, and secrets. Share it with me." He looked away. "I had meant to ask before, and then at your test, but then..." he trailed off.

"But—Origon." Rilan was speechless for a moment. "What about everything here?" Her hands took in not just the apartment, but the Nether itself. "I am only a majus as of today. I have to..."

"Have to what? Be finding a profession to please the people of the Great Assembly? Scraping your nose on the ground before the Council? Solving petty problems?"

The speaker's words about skirting the rules came back to her. "The Council is there for a reason," she answered, her voice hotter than she meant. "It directs the maji how to best help all of us."

Origon made a rude noise. "They are being a bunch of blowhards. What better time to see the universe? Come with me."

"This isn't an idle jaunt. Your own brother was killed!" Rilan stepped forward and poked him in the chest again. The man was still in denial.

"Well, yes." She caught another flash of sadness, but Origon was fast hiding it, becoming his usual blustery self. She knew if he didn't let it out now, it would come out later.

"Let us adventure through the jungles of Festuour. Even if I am not discovering what happened, it will be a time of solitude, and reflection."

"Solitude? With me in tow?"

"Reflection, then."

"You're impossible." But now the thought nagged at her. What would she do here? Wait until Vethis tested up to antagonize her? Find some psychologist to work with, using the House of Healing to diagnose petty issues in ten different species? Deal with stares from those who knew about her and Origon? She hadn't thought news of their relationship had spread that far. Vethis knew, of course, because all through university he made it his business to know anything that might be damaging to her image. Maybe he had spread it around in hopes of sabotaging her test.

And if she hung around the Nether, when would she get to see the homeworlds like she wanted?

"You are wanting to. I can tell."

"I...do." The words felt almost dragged from her, yet she found they were true. "But I have responsibilities here. And your brother..."

"I will be welcoming the help, and your responsibilities can wait for a time, can they not?"

"Well...yes."

"Do this for me. Come with me this one time. I will show you all I have lectured about in your classes, all I have told you of when we met alone. See if this is what you are wanting to do with your life." He paused, watching his hands for a moment before looking up at her. "With our lives." Once again, he looked vulnerable. "You will be...helping me past this period. And if you find it is not to your tastes, then come back here and find another path."

Rilan searched Origon's face, but she could feel the certainty bubbling up within her. Maybe she *could* help distract him, at least for the moment. Slowly, she leaned forward, lips close to his, and turned her head so she didn't bump his long nose.

They kissed, and Rilan pushed him back into the horrible yellow couch.

Some time later, Origon set the ottoman back aright, while Rilan picked up several of his little knick-knacks that had been knocked off.

"I am assuming that was a 'yes?'" Origon didn't take his eyes from a small rip in the hem of the ottoman.

"I only need to get a few things from my apartment—or Majus Meyta's apartment, rather." She adjusted a painting of a distinguished Kirian hanging above an ornamental side table. "What time is it, anyway?"

Origon squinted through to his kitchen, which had a small outside window—a testament to his ability to complain until he got what he wanted. He ran long fingers down his drooping moustaches. "It is looking to be around second lightening."

Rilan groaned. "I need some sleep, especially if we'll be up at fifth or sixth lightening."

Origon raised a feathery eyebrow, like an angular caterpillar over his eye. "There is my bedroom. You do not want to be disturbing your mentor at this hour."

"I suppose not." And it wasn't like the bed was any different than the... She looked at the couch. And the floor. And ottoman. Then her glance caught a picture of Origon and another Kirian—she assumed his brother—on the mantle, and she cringed.

"Really, are you sure? I shouldn't have... I didn't mean to take advantage of you right after..." She trailed off.

Origon actually laughed. It was a welcome sound. "I will be letting you know the first time you are taking advantage of *me*." His face grew serious. "Please. Come be with me for a little while longer. I will be welcoming the company. It is...helping while I cannot do anything else."

She followed Origon to his bedroom.

Rilan stretched, and looked out the window beside the bed. She swished her legs under the covers. Had she known he had silk sheets, she would have tried this earlier. Origon was up already, puttering in his washroom. He did seem to be better for having her sleep—and they did actually sleep this time— next to him. She listened to sounds of running water and questioned whether there was anything else that would have helped Origon deal with his grief in a better way. He was a complex man. Finally, she gave up the thought. Time would tell.

Without us, there could be no Great Assembly of Species, Speaker Karendi had said. Was she doing the right thing, going with him? What would her mentor say when she packed a few changes of clothes and left the apartment empty until she and Origon returned? When would that be? Days? Weeks? Yes, she deserved a vacation after studying for so long. She had finished both her testing and her graduation from university less than a ten-day apart. Not many did that. Yes, she could afford time off before transitioning to the life of a majus, and an apprentice psychologist. She already had recommendations to several places that might accept her. Would the lost time hurt her? Probably not. But on the other hand, was she just doing this to skirt the rules, like the speaker had said?

"Are you ready?" Origon poked his head out of the washroom.

"Just a moment," she answered, rolling out of his bed and pushing her rambling thoughts to the back of her mind.

They went out for breakfast. She strolled next to Origon, matching his long strides with quicker steps. It was a clear day in the Nether, bright and warm, with the light cascading down on them from the great walls. She looked across their length to where they met above the palace and Great Assembly, like some giant had shoved two slabs of translucent marble together. The walls, the same crystal substance as the columns, disappeared overhead, out of the range of her vision. Just as someday she would visit all ten homeworlds, someday she would travel to the top of the Nether. There were stories of course, but no one had ever brought back proof of what was up there, higher even than the birds and beasts flew. She had to make time to do those things. Otherwise she would be pinned to one place for the rest of her life.

"You are sure about this?" Origon brought her focus down to the ground. The area around the Spire of the Maji and between the houses of the maji encircling it was the largest continuous green plot in the Imperium. It was decorated with trees and bushes and tended by an army of groundskeepers. Specially trained birds and beasts prowled its circumference, never leaving the influence of the maji. It was far different from the warren of buildings that made up the rest of the Imperium.

"I'm surer by the minute," she answered. She pushed down a twinge of panic. It was just the feeling of worms in her belly because she was doing something new.

And totally insane.

"Is your brother in Martflen?" She redirected her thoughts.

"His body is, though I am not knowing how he was caught in such a place, especially to inconvenience me with having to travel there and finish his business." She snuck a glance at his face, but his expression—and crest—was carefully controlled. She wouldn't see another display like last night.

They walked in silence the rest of the way to the restaurant, a little corner establishment tucked between two busy thoroughfares and across from the campus of the medical research center. On the way, Rilan was almost positive she saw Vethis walking next to the hairy mass of a Festuour, possibly the same one as from last night. She shook her head. The oily man wasn't worth the effort. She needed to get him out of her head. Just wait and see if he passed his second testing.

The owner of the restaurant, a Lobath, lived above it and beneath a higher roadway serviced by the Imperium tram line.

"Come in, come in," Methle a'Tru, the owner, enthused at them when they opened the door. "Finally a majus, then? Will I expect more or less business from you in the future?" He kept up his steady flow of one-sided conversation, large silvery eyes staring unblinkingly as his head-tentacles twitched with delight. Methle had served generations of apprentices and maji.

Rilan and Origon got their usual—her, a fruit yogurt and spiced flatbread, and he a bowl of wiggling worms, with a tall container of hot tea. They discussed the logistics of getting to Festuour later that morning. Rilan watched the older man, his pointed features relaxed as he ate. Was this really the beginning of something lasting, or just a young woman's crush? She feared she was over-analyzing, but he was the one pushing for her to come. He wouldn't do that if he thought she was a mere fling, would he?

His brother's death certainly weighed on him. She wanted to help him—draw the pain from him, but she knew it would take time. Though she had known him for several cycles, much of Origon's past was still a mystery to her. Maybe she would learn more on this trip. She hoped so.

Afterwards, they stood outside the restaurant. "I'll meet you at the portal ground," she told him.

"I can easily be coming with you," he said. "I can help you carry your bags."

"I'll be traveling light," Rilan told him. Since when did Origon offer to carry someone else's things? "You just wait at the portal ground."

"You are sure? It is no problem."

"Quite." She searched his face, but could find no hint of amusement. His crest was calm, at ease.

As if telling her mentor—former mentor—that she was off on a wild adventure with one of the Council's least favorite maji wasn't bad enough. She shuddered to think about Origon being there.

"I am thinking Farha Meyta will not be minding much if I just—"

"Go." Rilan pointed away. Now she saw the crease next to his eyes. The Shiv-cursed man was laughing at her! He brushed his moustaches down, obviously hiding a smile.

She waited while he sauntered off, whistling through his pointy teeth, before she went in the other direction, toward the House of Healing. At least he felt better enough this morning to joke. She didn't think his humor would continue when they got to Martflen.

Majus Meyta was not at home—praises to all the gods— and she hurriedly packed what she needed. That only meant she looked more like she was running away when the door opened. Rilan's eyes darted around, but she knew there was no other exit. He must have been out at breakfast too.

"Have you found an apartment already?" her former mentor asked, removing his bowler hat and setting it on the stand next to the door. His tufts of white hair stood out like errant vegetation.

"Not...exactly."

Farha Meyta only raised his eyebrows, his face bland— an expression she knew from long experience meant, 'Yes? Tell me more.'

"I'm taking a quick vacation before starting my career as a majus."

"I see. With Origon Cyrysi, I suppose?"

Her mouth worked, but no sound came out.

"The Council will not be happy with this." His tone said he wasn't pleased either.

"It's only a few days. The Council doesn't need to know. I'll be back and starting my promising career before they figure anything out." She was babbling, but Majus Meyta had a certain way of looking at people.

"Hm." His mouth tightened, just a little.

Rilan took that as a form of acceptance and scurried past him to the door.

"Majus Ayama." The new title brought her up short. She looked back over a shoulder.

"I assume he wouldn't be satisfied with just visiting your home city or some other part of Methiem. Where are you going, if I may ask?"

She paused, but she owed him that much. "Festuour."

"Wear the bell I gave you. No knowing what diseases you could pick up on the first trip to another homeworld. I won't be there to heal you like when you decided to tangle with that nest of ratwolves in Low Imperium. And healing yourself is not your best skill, as we both know."

"Yes sir."

"On your way then." Rilan fled. Old obediences died hard.

The Spire of the Maji was the center of their presence in the Nether, surrounded by all six houses, and it had its own private portal ground, used almost exclusively by the maji. The ground was enclosed by an oasis of hedges and trees, obstructing the view of the rest of the city. When maji traveled there, it was like they were stepping out into a well-manicured estate, not a city crawling with millions.

This portal ground, just as with every other one on every homeworld, was tended by a majus, one of the less glorious jobs of the maji. Just as any majus, no matter which house, could create a portal, so everyone took their turn to tend them.

Origon was waiting. This early in the day there were few travelers, and a Benish majus she didn't recognize was tending the ground. The massive creature's skin had the hue of polished oak, and it stood three times as wide as she, though only slightly taller.

"There is no portal ground near Martflen," Origon told her. "The nearest is to be a week's journey away. I was given the information for the town's location, so I will be providing it to the majus. Do you have all you need?"

"I'm ready," Rilan said. She took the little white bell out of a pocket in her leather vest. Did it need to be touching her skin to work? Majus Meyta hadn't told her.

Origon went to the Benish, who watched him with pupil-less yellow eyes from a craggy face. Rilan followed.

"We are going to a location on Festuour," he told the Benish. "I will be communicating the exact coordinates, by your leave."

The Benish nodded its head with a creak. "This one will accept the information."

Origon raised a hand, the yellow of the House of Communication visible in rings around it. His house was the best at transferring the half scientific, half intuitive coordinates to make a portal reaching across the universe. One could only make a portal to where one had been, unless the location was transferred in this manner. So information about the maji's network of portals spread through their ranks.

Origon's hand touched the Benish's head, and the color moved from his hand to the other's craggy skin as he adjusted the Symphony of Communication. Rilan could not hear the change, of course, any more than she could hear the Symphony of any other house. The Benish's eyes dimmed at the wash of new information.

"This one has the location," it confirmed, and turned to the center of the ground. Thick arms with skin like old bark lifted and before them, a hole, pitch black, appeared in the air. As all maji shared the ability to make portals, Rilan caught hints of the melody of this place merging with another one: humid and dappled with light.

The hole, ringed in the blue of the House of Grace and a drab rust color, grew until it would accept Origon's height. Rilan pushed away the twinge of panic that always rose when she approached one of the pitch black holes between locations. She had to trust the majus who made the portal.

"Let us be going." Origon stepped into the blackness of the portal without even blinking.

Rilan gave the Benish a little wave, sighed, and entered after him.

FESTUOUR

- Festuour is almost an anomaly among the ten homeworlds with its dense air and crushing weight. Where one would feel light and graceful on Etan, that same person would drag their feet on the Festuour homeworld. Perhaps this is why it is inhabited by such fearsome predators. In contrast, the folk of this homeworld tend to be lighthearted, inquisitive, and jovial.

Excerpt from "A Dissertation on the Ten Species, Book IV: Festuour"

Rilan's foot hit the dirt with more force than she expected. She turned, clumsy, just in time to see the portal close behind them. The blue and rust rings around it compressed, squeezing it into a droplet, and then to nothing at all. Behind where it vanished, trees filled the sky.

Rilan adjusted her shirt, dark green under her leather vest. Both hung heavily on her. She was lighter in the Nether than on her home world of Methiem. But this was like walking with a heavy bag slung around her waist. The heat didn't help. It was almost as oppressive as her extra weight. It hung over her.

There was no breeze to lessen the heat, but there were trees everywhere—massive things, twice as wide as she was tall. Rather than the teaks, beeches, and banyans of her home, these had no leaves, but something like cilia in place of bark. Their branches divided like fingers, pointing nearly vertical. Small furry things nested in the branches, and glided from tree to tree.

"The town is to be this way."

As she turned, her loose black hair whipped her in the face. It was like little steel wires on this world.

"Phaw." She spit it out and went to draw it behind her back, but realized she still had something in her hand. The little bell. She looked back to Origon. He was pointing to a road cleared between the trees.

"Is it far?"

"A walk of a few minutes. I was placing the portal far enough from the town to be out of danger of passersby." There was a reason there were designated portal grounds.

"Then I'm putting my hair up in a braid while we walk. It feels like I have a bunch of wet socks tied to my head."

"My robes are being as much a bother." Today Origon wore orange and purple checks, with silver filigree and a green belt. A long collar stuck out behind his neck, but even it was drooping. It was very nearly coordinated colors, for a Kirian.

"You could always roll up your sleeves," Rilan suggested while they walked, "Show off a little arm." Origon scowled at her, making the ends of his moustaches twitch.

"There is no need to be indecent." But he swept a fold in the excess fabric of his robe and tucked it into his belt.

Soon they passed a massive wooden and metal construct ringed around a tree. The cilia-bark was stripped in thin spirals, leaving a fair bit still attached to the tree. Sheets of bark lay between massive swaths of oilcloth. Rilan spotted another scaffold, and another. Every alternate tree had something around it, though none seemed damaged or dying.

Festuour swarmed over the platforms, at least five to a tree. Most of the stocky furred creatures had iron-rimmed goggles and large wooden hats like circular shields. Besides that, they wore nothing but bandoliers filled with tools. They slotted curved spades in between the tree and its bark, and pulled off sloughs of material.

Rilan and Origon passed hundreds of trees being harvested before the dirt road dumped them into a bare expanse in the forest, holding a sizeable town. Rilan, her new braid in one hand, tied the little white bell to the tip with a bit of string she had in one pocket. It was almost impossible for a majus to see the glow of the House of Healing around it, it was so slight. She let it fall, like a pendulum down her back.

"Do you even know who we're meeting here?" she asked. Origon looked to her, his crest ruffling. The Nether didn't put the translation in her head on the homeworlds, of course, but she could tell curiosity in a Kirian.

"I am not certain. I am assuming a local law officer, if there is even one here." He looked around, arrogant as usual, no sign of his recent grief.

It was a funny thing, but maji, as if they carried a bit of the Nether around with them, had no trouble communicating with each other on the homeworlds, and she would be able to hear and translate the local language. Communicating *to* the non-maji inhabitants, on the other hand, was another matter. She ran through phrases in her head, hoping the Festuour in this little backwater town spoke the Trader's Tongue.

As they passed through, Rilan saw the town was laid out in a spiral, stores and warehouses on the outer arms nearest the trees they harvested, and residences in the middle. Anyone— or anything—coming out of the forest surrounding them would have to go through low, curved, wooden buildings containing tools easily adaptable to weaponry.

They saw no species but Festuour as they walked through the town, and the usually jolly creatures stared back suspiciously. Their brown and green fur looked bedraggled and matted in the humid heat. A mother in a frilly lace hat pulled her cub close to her as they passed, watching them through narrowed blue eyes behind spectacles. A male in a high top hat and monocle peered down his snout at them.

"Cheery lot," Rilan murmured. "This is a wonderful reception for my first visit to another homeworld."

Hantamoptigor Wint, Guarder

"I do not believe Festuour prefer this environment. They must live here for the textiles they make from the trees." Origon motioned to a factory as they walked by, stacks of the raw cilia-bark on one side, and folded sheets of sheer fabric on the other. They had passed several others like it.

The local law house was mid-way through the town, dividing the residences from the factories and stores. A large Festuour was standing outside, his protruding belly circumnavigated by a bandolier of pockets with paper, writing utensils, a short sword, and even a small projectile weapon—one of the newer ideas to come from Methiem. Rilan usually admired her homeworld's inventions, but not in this case. The slugs they shot moved so fast even a majus didn't have time to react. Maji were the servants and protectors of the Great Assembly. They should be harder to hurt than a non-majus.

"You all are here for the feather-head, I expect?" the Festuour drawled. He was wearing a large hat, the sides curled up and a metal emblem on the front. He was the local equivalent of the sheriff, Rilan guessed. The bit of the Nether left in her mind made his words clear, even if his body language was strange.

His blue eyes took in Origon. "No offense, meant, naturally."

Rilan watched her friend, noting the tightening of his mouth, the way his crest bunched and curled. Kirians in general were a stoic lot—but Origon was affected, not just by the epithet, but by the reminder of his brother's death, she guessed. She put a hand on his sleeved arm, but he didn't look at her.

"I am Origon Cyrysi," he said, and there was a yellow aura around him, more concentrated about his throat. He must have been putting his song into the Symphony of this place to make his words easier to understand. She would be able to comprehend him either way, so it was hard to tell if he was speaking in the Trader's Tongue.

The Festuour's bright eyes widened. He was one of the few of his species who didn't wear some form of spectacles. "And I'm Hantamoptigor Wint, Guarder. Then y'all're related, I reckon. About the only thing I've found out about this fellow is his name, and that has a 'Cyrysi' in it too."

Origon nodded, and Rilan heard his sharp teeth grind together beneath his moustache. The aura was still around him. "He is to be my brother. Delphorus Cyrysi."

"Yep. That's the name he gave us, when he was still alive. Best you folks come in. We've got him laid out." The sheriff turned his bulk through an arched doorway, waving a three-fingered paw lazily over his shoulder.

Rilan tried to catch Origon's arm as they went inside, to say something—anything—to show she would support him, but he brushed past her, his crest twitching.

The inside of the law house was sparse, but clean. Wint took them through several rooms with various desks, piles of paper, wooden cabinets, and Festuour clerks scribbling notes.

In the back of the building was a closed and locked door. Wint produced a ring of circular keys from a pouch on his bandolier and unlocked it.

"In here. We keep a special room for any dead in our town. Got to keep 'em chill, on account of the heat here. Turns 'em to slush otherways."

The room was freezing. Rilan's eyes automatically went to several devices fastened to the ceiling, walls, and floor. They were small bundles of wire, with an aura of blue, orange, and brown around them. The Houses of Grace, to control the humidity, Power, to control the heat, and Potential, to fashion the artifact. Physically the wires glowed a soft yellow-red, melting the ice that gathered around them. They were hot, busy removing the heat and humidity from the air.

Delphorus Cyrysi was laid out on a wooden table in the middle of the room, and Origon was already at his side. The body was still dressed in a dull brown robe—the least colorful she had seen on a Kirian. It was filled with pockets, inside and out, and a line of Kirian hieroglyphics was stitched on the right breast, probably giving his name. Rilan stuck her hands in her pockets to warm them.

She could see similarities in the face—the long nose, and triangular feathered eyebrows—though Delphorus hadn't worn a moustache. His face was relaxed in death, but Origon's was fixed. He gently ran his liverspotted hands down his brother's robe, as if looking for something.

"His work as an officer was meaning much to him. Female Kirians were never holding much interest for him. We were alike in some ways." He gave her a shaky smile, filled with sharp teeth. It didn't reach his eyes.

"Y'all lookin' for this?" Wint held up a leather-bound book. "He requested some help on a case of his, even though I told him this was a smidge out of his jurisdiction. He wouldn't listen and went off into the jungle." The sheriff shook his head, blue eyes fixed on Origon. "One of the harvesters found him a couple days later, sprawled out. He was dead, but still fresh. No animals got to him. That's when we sent off a message to his kin. Guess it found you."

Origon took the book, slowly opening it.

"Can I?" Rilan gestured toward the body. Investigating it—him—felt wrong, but it was the only way she could think to help. At least she might be able to determine what happened. Origon waved a hand at her to proceed and she went to the table.

She closed her eyes and delved into the Symphony. Near the top were the reactions in her body, and those in Origon's and the Festuour's. She mentally pushed those aside and listened deeper. Everything organic in the room had some signature, but now that Delphorus was dead it was harder to find his song instead of that of the wooden table he lay on. Every living—and once living—thing had one. Maji were just able to tap into theirs.

There.

Signs of decay permeated already, even in the chilly room. Parts of the song that once defined him were missing, or breaking down, with notes and phrases dissonant. But that wasn't what killed him. She was looking for something specific, violent. An animal attack, or a natural occurrence. It should show up in the Symphony, but there was nothing.

"I can't find how he was killed," she said.

"What's she sayin'?" The Festuour cocked an ear at her. She had forgotten to speak in the Trader's Tongue. It was so natural in the Nether simply to speak in her native language. She tried again.

"I..not am...finding death cause..." She spoke in broken phrases.

"I don't think he died of a cold, girlie, if that's what you're trying to say." Wint squinted at her.

Rilan tried not to get frustrated. "I said he has no having any wounds."

Wint just looked confused. "No what now? Why would he do that?"

"Wounds!"

"He was insulted?"

She growled in annoyance. "Origon?"

But Origon was staring at his brother's body. She touched his shoulder and he jumped.

"She means my brother was not killed in a manner that is obvious."

"Well why didn't she say so?" Wint scratched at his snout. "I could have told you that. Don't know what he died from, and we'd rather not have a big incident in our little town. We're quiet here. Don't like folks from the big city coming down, messing things up. Figured we could handle it quiet-like." He gestured to Delphorus' notebook. "Don't have a translator 'round here for Kirian languages, neither."

Origon looked down at the notebook, still open in his hand. It was filled with the same style hieroglyphics as were stitched into Delphorus' robe. If they were still in the Nether, Rilan would have been able to read them with the aid of its translation. Her friend didn't look like he was taking in any of the words.

"What does it say?" she prompted.

Origon started again. "It is to be his journal log," he said. The yellow aura still hung at his throat. He was not taking his brother's death well. She thought it was just his normal aloofness, back at his apartment in the Nether, but now she could tell he was shaken. If his concentration slipped enough, his change to the Symphony might reverse, and then he wouldn't be able to reproduce it until either some time had passed, or they moved a distance through the town. It would take even longer to find what they needed from Wint. She needed to get him away from here.

"Maybe there's something later in the book," Rilan suggested gently. "Perhaps near the end." Origon was holding it open at the front, where presumably it held some sort of identification of his brother.

He grunted, crest flat and unmoving, and flipped through the log. Several minutes passed, and Rilan tried not to fidget. Her teeth were starting to chatter with the cold. She didn't look at the sheriff, though she knew the Festuour was watching them. It was best for Origon to come to terms with this on his own, but they needed some information on what happened.

"He was investigating," Origon said finally. His face showed a little more animation as he read. "There were to be several homicides in his jurisdiction on Bhuontifontona—the capitol of our home province." He turned a page. "All victims were displaying the same identifying marks—strange circular wounds in their heads and necks." He looked through a few more pages. "He was suspecting a Festuour, for some reason. It does not say why. He traced the suspect's movements to near this town, bought passage through the nearest portal ground, and traveled here, one ten-day ago."

"That tells me what I needed, folks," Wint said, unheeding of Origon's state. "There was a madman brought down in a big city up north, just after he got here." He waved a paw at the table, "That must've been who he was looking for, but he went the wrong direction in his investigation and ran himself afoul of something local that didn't agree with him. We have a mighty dangerous world for those unfamiliar."

But that didn't make sense. Only an idiot would go to a little manufacturing village when their target was in a larger metropolis. Origon's relatives might be arrogant, but she doubted they were stupid. Had Delphorus found some other clue?

She was about to argue with Wint, who obviously wanted them out of his quiet town with the least fuss, and didn't particularly care about Kirians, when Origon turned back to his brother on the table, gently arranging his robe. He was in no state to reach logical conclusions.

"So will ya'll be takin' the body back with you?" Wint asked.

"Give us one moment," Rilan said, slowly enunciating her words so Wint could understand her poor speech. He nodded.

"Origon, tell him you need to make an offering to your ancestors over your brother's body," she said, in her native tongue.

"But I do not practice…" he cut off at her glare, blinked, and repeated her words to the sheriff. At least he was together enough to take her hint.

The Festuour exhaled a cloud of mist. "Don't take long now. It's cold in here." He shut the door behind him.

"What were you—" Origon looked more clearheaded.

"There's something wrong here. I couldn't find how your brother was…what happened to him." She went back to the table. "The portal ground is up there, so why would he come down here if the one he was after was in the city up north? He must have had some other objective."

Origon cocked his head to the side. "You are correct. See if you are being able to find anything else," he gestured to his brother's body.

She leaned close to Delphorus, searching deep into the Symphony. It resisted, as she had done the same thing just recently. But she hadn't actually used her song to make a change, so it was possible to perform the same action. There was no sign of trauma in the body's past, and she searched deeper, to where the Symphony divided into smaller and smaller parts, like repeating solos that made up the body. Something was off at this level. Parts of the music seemed to be missing, as if Delphorus' life had been leeched away. The music felt wrong, as if it had been...

"Origon," she said. He looked at her, catching her mood. "Can the House of Power tell you how his life energy was connected to his body? I think something stole it."

He moved slowly, looking thoughtful, paused, then, reached out with long fingers to hover over his brother's chest. His face was set in a frown. An orange aura appeared, moving down from his fingertips to the body's chest. Origon was using his secondary house. Those maji's specialty was to hear how the Symphony connected one thing to another.

The orange glow spread to Delphorus' body, as Origon closed his eyes, tilting his head as if listening intently. Finally, he opened them again.

"There are to be changes, very deep in the Symphony. The way my...the way this body was connected together has been changed at a basic level."

"That's what I suspected. I think your brother was killed by a majus." Rilan held his eyes for a long moment. "We need to find who did this."

Origon nodded in agreement. "For more than one reason." His face was dark.

Rilan almost expected the cold surface of the door to resist her as she pushed, but it opened easily, and they exited into the hot and humid interior of the law office.

The big Festuour was holding a sheaf of paper over his belly, a length of charcoal gripped in his paw. "We can pack that body up for y'all, if you like. Just give us an address. I'm assuming y'all came from the Nether, seein' as you're maji. We can request a special portal for it."

"Thank you," Rilan told him slowly, since Origon was silent. "But we will come tomorrow. Tonight, we must find lodgings."

Wint's long snout lowered and his charcoal drooped in disappointment. "Ah—of course. The Harvester's Stump can offer accommodation. Tomorrow, then? We're a quiet town, best to button this all up before it causes more hubbub around here."

Maybe the sheriff's idea of a "hubbub" was different than hers. Rilan thought for a moment, but her language skills weren't up to the task. She whispered to Origon, who translated, the glow still hanging around his neck.

"Are there any local maji in Martflen?"

Wint looked confused for a moment. "Just you two. The nearest is up north, and she only makes an appearance here once in a bear's age." He frowned. "Haven't seen her for about three cycles now, in fact."

"And in which direction was my brother's body found?"

Wint frowned, but pointed across the town with his charcoal. "East of town, right where the forest starts. Why do you ask?"

Rilan waved the question away, smiled at him tightly, and dragged Origon with her out of the law office. She hoped she hadn't given the sheriff any offense while she was here. She couldn't remember nuances of Festuour body language. How did people live outside the Nether? No wonder one didn't see alien species on other homeworlds often.

Once in the street, they turned in the direction the sheriff pointed.

"We can be purchasing a room at the local common house later." Origon said. "I want to see the place where it happened."

"Yes. Something's off here." She walked along beside him, shorter legs taking more steps to keep up with his stride.

"Are you thinking Wint is keeping something back?"

"No," she answered slowly. "I think he really is just trying to protect his little town from scandal. I don't think he knows about this other majus."

Origon looked back to the law office, stopping in the middle of the street.

"There's nothing you can do for your brother now," Rilan insisted. "But you can honor him by finding out why he's on that table." She had to keep him moving or he would stop like he did in the morgue.

"They'll thank us after we bring back the majus responsible for this. Come on. You love wandering out in the wild. It will help you feel better." She caught one of his hands, his long curved nails sliding along her skin; hard, and with an edge. She pulled, and finally he came with her. They headed through the town.

They stopped in a general store on the way out, at her insistence. Origon would have been happy to go off into the forest with nothing at all, but she wanted supplies. The Festuour had always been allies to her species, and over the cycles, there had been cross-pollination of foods and other cultural likes. That meant she could find dried jerky to eat. She also bought several canteens of fresh water, rope, and a pack to carry them in. She even found a folding tent, but Origon stopped her from buying that for some reason. She was surprised how little it cost. This town must have been poorer than she thought. She used only a few small clear chips of the

Nether's currency, and still got several sticks of local currency back in change.

Soon after leaving the store, they faced a wall of the cilia-bark trees. The town was not that large. "You will be more tired for carrying that pack," Origon told her. His voice was the one he adopted lecturing to freshmen, and Rilan rolled her eyes. She had it strapped to her back, her leather vest providing some padding between the rough fabric of the pack and her linen shirt. The yellow glow had faded from his throat sometime in the past few minutes as he reversed the change he made to his speech and reabsorbed the notes of his song. They shouldn't need translation in the woods.

"I'll be fine. You just worry about helping me track where Delphorus went." She knelt down at the treeline, hands just above the ground. Chords and whole musical phrases of the Symphony flew past her, containing the many biological changes in the forest. There were numerous creatures hidden around them. However, there had not been harvesters at these trees recently, so any sentient disturbance would stand out. People made their own very definite impact on the music of the universe. She used her song to make a minor chord major and the differences popped to the forefront. There was something to their left, and she went that direction, Origon following.

They went a few hundred paces. "Here. There's a footprint." It was partially buried in the dusty shavings the trees dropped from the end of their cilia—probably some form of waste product. She reclaimed her notes and the obvious signs faded from her perception. No matter, they had the trail now. "What can you find?"

Origon bent down next to her, the orange glow of the House of Power already forming about his arms as he laid his hand in the footprint. It had been made by the large three-toed foot of a Festuour, facing toward town. The aura transferred to the footprint, tracing the outline, uncovering how this one piece was connected to its surroundings. Two orange lines spread from the print, one back to the town, the other into the woods, outlining another footprint nearby.

"This way." Origon stood, still concentrating on the ground. Rilan followed, watching her friend for any sign of distress. Yes, tracking work would be good for him. It would keep him busy.

They followed the footprints backwards, until they reached a larger disturbance, not far into the treeline. The ground was trampled, and several of the trees had patches of bark scraped off.

"This is to be the place." Origon rolled his shoulders, and the orange glow disappeared again, reabsorbed.

"Can you figure out what happened, or is that too similar for another change to the Symphony?" Rilan asked, referring to tracking the footprints.

Origon drew up, lifting his long nose, ends of his moustaches twitching. "Of course I can be figuring out what happened. I was tracking through the wilds of the homeworlds—"

"While I was still a child. You don't need to remind me how much older you are." It was somewhat of a sore point to her, but Origon didn't seem to notice. He blinked at her blankly.

"Never mind. Go on." Rilan waved a hand at their surroundings. She was trying too hard to keep him busy, to not think about his brother, and it was showing. Origon mumbled something, his crest rippling. He went to a nearby tree, listening, then made a tying motion with his hands. As he left one tree to go to another, strands of yellow light fluttered as if a breeze were blowing them, but it was not the same slight breeze that blew through the trees today. The etheric light fluttered to a different wind. He went from tree to tree, and the light trailed after him as if he were making a giant spider web of ribbons. Soon all the nearby surfaces were covered, strands of light all shifting and pointing in the same otherworldly breeze.

Origon stepped back, cocking his head, as if observing the streamers of light. "It is not to be complete. Can you tell exactly where my…the body was found?"

Rilan watched what he was doing. She knew he was very good with the House of Communication, which the yellow ribbons indicated. He was harnessing wind currents of some sort, she thought, but didn't know for what purpose. Still, she nodded and knelt, hands out again. The Symphony resisted.

She couldn't make the same change she had to discover the footprint. It was a novice mistake. She should have held on to the change instead of letting it go the first chance she got. She shook her head, frustrated with herself.

After a moment, she listened to her own Symphony, using a few notes of her song to increase her sense of smell. The faded scents of the Festuour harvesters appeared as large hazy masses in the air. The body was easy to find as well, especially since it didn't move on its own.

Origon's brother. Not just a body. But she pushed the thought away. Find the answers first.

"It was right here." She outlined where Delphorus had fallen, one arm outstretched. She sniffed. "There were four Festuour as well." She waved her hands to indicate where they would have gathered around Delphorus.

Origon nodded, laying a hand in the center of each of the masses, then wordlessly touching the center of where his brother's body lay with one finger.

The ribbons of light around them flapped crazily in a nonexistent wind, then died, then flapped again, and the streamers lengthened and joined together. Rilan stepped back, trying to see what Origon had done.

The streamers of light outlined a scene frozen in time, a body made of yellow light laying on the ground and four larger shapes around it, identifiable as the outlines of Festuour. They were frozen in the act of gesturing to each other and to

Delphorus. No lines passed through the phantom bodies. Origon had mapped the air itself in that moment in time.

"That's incredible," Rilan breathed. "How did you learn..." But Origon walked past her, to another shape, vaguer than the others, captured as it hid behind a tree, observing. It was on all fours.

Rilan raised her head and sniffed. "Someone, or something, was here with them."

"The majus?" Origon cocked his head, watching the fuzzy shape.

"I...don't know. The smell is heavy, almost like an animal."

"It came from deeper in the forest, in this direction." Rilan pointed, and Origon raised a hand and twisted. The yellow streamers moved along their paths, creating a funnel aimed farther into the woods.

They moved in that direction, Origon controlling his captured breeze. While walking, Rilan sank farther into the detritus of the trees than expected, and she slowed her pace. No sense tripping over a root and breaking her leg on this heavy world. The woods were strange. Unlike the forests of her home where many types of trees grew together, this forest was all cilia-bark trees, branches like reaching fingers. Rilan wondered if it was planted or if the trees pushed out any other organism. Light got to the ground, but aside from a few scrubby bushes here and there, nothing grew underneath. The floor of the forest was deep with the shaving-like waste of the trees.

There was animal life hiding nearby, despite the lack of leaves or ground cover. She caught glances of the same gliding creatures they saw on the way in, and once in a while saw a tuft of fur or tail of ground creatures the size of the forest cats they had back near her home city. These seemed skittish and were camouflaged, and Rilan guessed they were prey creatures, not predators, even though they were rather large.

Every so often, Origon paused for a few minutes while touching a tree, mapping another point in the complex web of air movement he was building. Sometimes she saw the shapes of animals outlined in the false breeze. Once or twice she saw a man-sized shape. Was he going farther back in time, mapping the air around where his brother had walked?

Rilan kept the change to her sense of smell, though she felt it wearing on her. Holding a change contrary to the Grand Symphony of the universe took effort. Many other new maji would be struggling more than she did. Take that oaf Vethis, for example. Well, he wouldn't even be out here in the first place.

Origon was sweating, and she watched a bead of water roll into his feathery moustache. It wasn't just the humidity. If it was hard for her, it was amazing he could hold such a complex change over this length of time. She rarely had a chance to observe how talented he was, especially with the

House of Communication, and it gave her new appreciation for the tests the house heads set for her. Of course she had been meant to pass them. Otherwise she would have had no chance.

"How long can you hold on to the air map?" she asked. They were already some distance away from the source of the change and traveling farther by the moment.

"Long enough." The terseness of his speech spoke volumes. She let the matter drop as a scent caught at her.

"What's that?" It was sharp, and pungent. Similar to the smell at the site of the disturbance, but from a different individual. She couldn't place it. It wasn't the musty scent of the ground creatures.

"There are predators on Festuour," Origon said, watching her sniff the air. "On this homeworld, the dominant species is having a massive build, thick fur to repel fangs and claws, and a mouth full of sharp teeth. Imagine what their wild fauna is like."

Rilan was leading, and forced her Kirian friend to stop as she slowed. "You decided to mention this only after we entered the deep dark forest without telling anyone where we were going?"

Origon shrugged. "It was to be your idea."

Rilan growled. "You are—" *Arrogant. Stuck up. A thrill seeker.* "—going to take the first watch when we camp for the night."

It was getting dark, and her change to the Symphony was progressively harder to maintain. The longer she used her new sense of smell, the more likely she wouldn't be able to reverse the change, and thus lose those notes from her song forever as the change became permanent. There was a good reason she didn't have the sense of smell of a dog. It would mess up her other senses, eventually.

She knew Origon was suffering, though he would never admit it.

"Let's find somewhere to stop."

They walked until they found a space between the ever-present cilia-barked trees large enough to camp for the night. Origon touched one last trunk, watched how the line of yellow streamers blew, and nodded to himself. The yellow light vanished from around them and he stood straighter, as if putting down a rucksack full of bricks.

Rilan reversed her own change and felt the notes of her song come back to her. It was never completely perfect—one always lost one or two in the transition—but it was much less than if she had made the change permanent. She'd feel better tomorrow.

She took in a long breath of the warm, humid air, and began making a little bed among the roots of one of the trees, grumbling about Origon keeping her from getting a tent. It wouldn't have cost much more.

"What are you to be doing?" She turned to find his head cocked to one side.

"I'm trying to make a place to sleep, since someone insisted we didn't need tents." She stood, and put her hands on her hips.

"That is to be solved easily." Origon even gave her a little smile as he came over. He set his stance, feet planted firmly, and raised both hands. Yellow and orange auras, mixing together like pools of paint, extended from his outstretched hands. She could tell he was listening intently. He shook his hands and the aura flexed out like a sheet. It fell slowly, draping over an area big enough for two people to sleep comfortably together. As if there was a tent pole, the center hung in the air, the sides of the sheet of aura draping to the ground, the back of it resting against the tree she had chosen.

Rilan raised her eyebrows. She didn't know he could do that. Being born with access to more than one house invited combinations she had never really considered.

"What is it?" she asked.

"It is the mixture of air and heat, compressed to be forming a tactile surface." He brought a fist down on the surface, invisible to non-maji except for a faint glimmer in the air. Something resisted him.

"And you can hold that all night?" And after mapping miles of air currents, too.

"It is staying in one place. I will be nearby. It is no matter."

Rilan ducked under the sheet of compressed air. Origon had left an entrance, clearly visible to a majus by a break in the yellow and orange aura. She lay back on the ground, her pack making a suitable pillow against the tree base. Shavings drifted down from the tree above her, and gently landed on the invisible surface above. There would be a thin layer by the morning, she expected. At least they wouldn't be on her.

Origon took first watch, sitting outside the impromptu tent. Rilan watched the unfamiliar stars, trying to find similarities. Festuour was the closest homeworld to her own, but she could find none of the constellations she knew.

She was almost asleep when Origon began to speak.

"I was always closest to Delphorus, out of all of my family members." Rilan propped herself up on elbows, leaning forward to hear better. He didn't look at her, but she saw the outline of his head turn in the darkness. He knew she was listening.

"Neither of us got along with the rest. Our grandmother was being an eminent stateswoman in her youth, and expected her descendants to be following in her trail. My father, her son, was deeply religious, and was trained in the priesthood, leading the family in their regard of our ancestors. He was using his talent for speech, but not in the manner my grandmother preferred. She never had any regard for our mother. When I was found to be able to hear the Grand Symphony, I was sent to the Nether, of course, for training. I could only be accessing the House of Communication then. My second house, that of Power, came later. I think my grandmother expected me to be serving on the Council in a few cycles. She was disappointed.

"Delphorus was younger than me. He showed no inclination for the maji or for public speech, which as you know is highly prized on Kiria." He waved a shadowy hand, as if the point was self-evident. Rilan crept closer to the entrance of the tent, pulling herself into a ball.

"The position of lawman, especially one devoted to ferreting out wrongdoers, is viewed as a necessary evil in my province, but is never a prestigious job anywhere on Kiria. When my brother chose such a base job, my grandmother was near to be disowning him. She died a few cycles after he started his profession." Origon's voice dipped alarmingly at the last sentence, and Rilan resisted the urge to hug the man. She wanted to hear more.

"He confessed to me later he felt he failed our family, though I never did." Origon left unsaid whether he considered himself a success. Rilan had an idea, considering his standing with the Council.

"We kept in contact, sending messages to each other about our work. I was visiting him when I had the chance, as he never had much money. My father joined the ancestors a few cycles after our grandmother and our mother was long departed. It was a sign of their feelings for us that the family house and all the accumulated wealth was left to the descendants of a cousin of our grandmother—a noted public speaker, I might be adding."

"That's awful," Rilan said. The shadow of Origon's head nodded. She saw his crest rise.

"It is to be somewhat traditional on Kiria, in our province."

Rilan moved out of the tent, snuggling up next to him, now that he seemed to be done with his story. One of the moons of Festuour was up, and she thought she could see tears on Origon's cheeks, reflecting its faint light.

"We had not spoken for several months before…before I got the communication."

Rilan touched his cheek, wiping a tear away. "I'm sorry," she said. She was an only child. "I can't imagine what it would be like to lose—"

Something cracked, above them and to the right.

"What was that?" Rilan searched the branches above them. She started to push up, but a shape dropped with a thud in front of Origon. The same sharp scent hit her, strong now, like metal and rotting meat.

"Back!" He pushed her and she fell against the sheet of air making their tent. It flexed slightly at her weight, and she slipped underneath it. Origon scooted in after her.

"Ancestor of a turtle!" he cursed. "I cannot be creating another shield over the entrance." His body was blocking a clear view of whatever was out there. In the dark, it was only a massive shape under the starlight. It stood over them, now they were inside the tent.

She saw the yellow of the House of Communication blossom in his hands, and a blast of air blew the scent of the thing out of the tent. There was a deep snort and the shadow shook its head, which seemed half as big as the tent. Something smashed against the sheet of air, pressing Origon back into her. He grunted and the colors intensified. He was putting more of his song into holding the change. She caught a glimpse of a massive razor-sharp claw bearing down on them. It ran over the top of the tent of air, the surface bowing alarmingly.

"That didn't do anything," she said. "How do we get rid of it?" She jumped as the creature grunted at them, loud and deep.

"I am open to any suggestions, provided they are quick." Origon scooted back farther as something swiped across the opening with a hiss of air.

"I can't see it clearly," Rilan said. "I don't know what its biology is, and I don't know how to affect it." The Symphony seemed remote and hard to hear. She had never been in a situation like this before. Even her testing had been a controlled environment. The beast swiped again and its sharp smell flowed back. It couldn't seem to figure out why something resisted it.

"I'm going to adjust my eyes," Rilan told Origon. It was the only thing she could think of. He only grunted, not turning. He was pressed into her, her back to the tree, her pack under her. The orange and yellow outline of the sheet of air was moving. He was trying to adjust it between them and the thing.

Rilan listened for the Symphony, but it was spotty and far away. She closed her eyes and focused on her own body, one of the easiest actions for her house.

Come on. Focus. She couldn't fail them now. She had tested under pressure a hundred times. Another deep grunt made her pop an eye open before closing it again.

She listened for the melody of her visual system. This was familiar. The tune floated by, faster than usual, in time with her heartbeat. Change the tempo slightly, use her song to adjust the cadence and brighten her night vision.

"I can see it now. Move out of the way." She peered past Origon, trying to get a good look at their attacker.

The second one landed on top of them.

Rilan looked up and screamed. Above her, two sets of serrated jaws sawed at the air inches above her face. She felt the sheet of air push her to the ground. Triangular teeth vied with three large tusks jutting at angles from a face that seemed half mouth. The shaggy body was larger than the now flat tent.

She flinched back into the ground, but its full weight was on them. She could barely see Origon, on his stomach beside her, not moving. The sheet of air above her pressed in, pushing both of them down into the ground. Jaws snapped so close above her she couldn't focus on them.

On the positive side, the other one couldn't get at them, now the opening was squashed flat.

Her arms were pinned, and Origon's face was being crushed into the debris of the forest floor. He wasn't moving, but he was breathing. Unconscious. His tent would only last a few minutes without him holding it in place. When it dissolved, there would be no barrier between her and the teeth above her.

This was not the time to crack under pressure.

Rilan closed her eyes again, and tried to ignore the wet sounds and grunts from above her. *Assess the situation. Make a decision. Follow through.* Words her mentor had taught her long ago snapped into her head.

She delved into the Symphony. There was no problem finding it this time. Pure adrenaline brought the music to her, beating in time with her fear. She blocked out the Symphonies of her body and Origon's, focusing on the two creatures. If she could only touch them, it would be easy. She could affect their bodies or minds, make them docile. But if she could touch them, they could touch her.

She concentrated on the pheromones traveling back and forth, along with grunts and snarls. They were a mated hunting pair, she realized.

She adjusted notes, hoping the sheet of air was porous enough to pass scents through. Copied pheromones might confuse them.

A few moments later, the snarling stopped and she cracked open an eye. The jaws were still, and the massive head was tilted, watching her. An eye the size of her fist took her in. Shaggy black hair surrounded it.

The pressure on her increased and another head joined the first, watching. She felt a root digging into her leg. Origon was pressed almost completely into the shavings.

There was no snarling now, but twice the weight—not the solution she wanted. The tent dissipated much of the creature's weight, or they would both be crushed to death. Still, the air was getting thick and her head felt fuzzy. She wouldn't get another chance. The next change had to be right.

She took back the notes of her song and searched the Symphony again for anything that would draw the beasts away. Free from the confusing pheromones, a paw the size of her chest bounced off the blanket of air, just above her. Rilan exhaled sharply as something gave with a muted crack. Probably a rib. Pain flooded through her.

Concentrate! She would not cry out.

She poured through the melodies. What were the strongest urges? Food and sex, and she was food. Sex, then. She grabbed at notes as they flew by, and missed more than she caught.

Change!

The Symphony resisted, but these pheromones were different from the last change. Finally, she captured enough of the notes to create a phrase of the music, and used her song to push it into place, melding it with the beast's natural instincts.

One of the creatures snorted in response, a massive blast of air. The other one cuffed it on its head and Rilan grunted when the pressure on her increased.

She realized she could feel fur tickling her wrist. The pressure was increasing because the blanket of air was dissolving. Her vision contracted to a tunnel.

Come on, take the bait.

The first beast sniffed in her direction, smelling alluring pheromones.

The second one swatted the first in the head again. It responded with a growl that shook her eardrums, but its head turned back to her.

A foot pressed her pelvis into the ground cover and her muscles protested. The blanket was going faster.

Another cuff, and this time the beast responded to its mate, stepping away to growl. The other growled back, and suddenly the weight was off her.

The ground shook as the two beasts cantered off into the woods, one chasing the other like cats the size of wagons. A nearby tree creaked as the first caught a low branch with wicked curved claws and pulled itself up. The second followed.

Rilan let out a breath, looked around with her augmented eyes, then turned to Origon. He wasn't breathing. She snaked an arm beneath him, pulled him around, and cried out as her rib protested.

Definitely broken.

She tried again, slower this time, and got him turned over, brushed shavings off his face and out of his moustaches. She knew basic medicine, but it wasn't her thing. Her forte was mental, not physical. Some of those in the House of Healing could repair flesh itself, though it was strangely not that common.

She pressed an ear to his chest. The heartbeat was strong, and fast. Kirians' hearts beat harder than her own species. So why wasn't he breathing?

She dived into the Symphony again, counting tempos to find the music of Origon's breath. A foreign melody clashed with the one that kept him alive.

An obstruction.

"Shiv's eyes," she swore, and hooked a finger past the Kirian's sharp teeth. She found the collection of tree shavings that was blocking his throat and pried them out. With a snort, Origon gasped in a breath.

Rilan inhaled, clutched a hand to her chest, and exhaled slowly, around her broken rib. *Only a majus would listen to the Symphony before checking to see if someone was choking.*

"What…is happening?" Origon's voice was weak and hoarse. Rilan took in their trampled supplies and the trees around them. The last yellow and orange of the tent faded as Origon reabsorbed its notes.

"Nothing I couldn't handle. I'll take the next watch." Origon snorted something, but was soon asleep, curled up in the tree roots.

Rilan watched the sky the rest of the night, thinking of what he told her about his brother. The forest sounds had returned to normal, but just in case, she copied the scent of the tree she rested against, replacing her own and Origon's so they didn't attract any more attention. And she kept the change to her eyes until just before the sun rose.

Origon was limping when they started out the next day, though he insisted he was fine. The extra weight on this world would not help his injury, or hers. They would be slower to heal. There was not much to do for her rib except to lace her leather vest as tight as she could. It still burned with every step, making it harder to breathe.

"My canteen is empty," he said, shaking his leather pouch.

"And mine spilled last night," Rilan answered. She closed her eyes and felt the Symphony of the forest spill past her, like a warm summer wind. The trees soaked up water stored beneath the ground, but they were better fed in one direction.

"This way. I think there's a stream nearby. We can both get more water."

"Were you hearing...ah...anything else?" Origon didn't look at her.

"There are no more of those creatures close." She answered his unasked question. "This ecosystem wouldn't be able to support many more of them anyway." She glanced to the trees where she could see bits of fur slide out of sight. The prey animals on the ground were well hidden.

The morning was still warm, and humid. Condensation beaded on the bark of the trees. The land rose gently as they made their way to the stream, and Origon was silent.

"I'm sorry," she finally said, trying to ignore the pain in her chest. Origon looked up.

"For what?"

She gestured at his leg. "I'm not very good with healing. It's like the notes just slide away when I try to do it. I can understand the music of a mental state, or a set of pheromones, or even change the way a body works, but to actually grow new cells?" She shook her head.

Origon shrugged. "Some are to be better at certain things. It is natural."

"It's about the only thing Vethis is good at," Rilan continued, hardly hearing her friend's response. "He always held that over me."

"Your testing rival? I am seeming to remember the two of you arguing through one of my classes."

Rilan snorted. "Rivals. He's the lazy son of rich parents. He had everything I didn't growing up. He barely got through University, and most of that was from cheating off his friends. Yet he tested with me. It's so rare to have the ability to change the Symphony, and it's wasted on him."

"But he can heal," Origon offered. "We are always needing good physicians." Rilan rolled her eyes.

"Yes, he's decent at it. He would be better if he practiced it rather than mooching off his parents."

"Surely he is to be proficient at some things."

Rilan waved the comment off. "Maybe, if he applied himself to them." She thought about their test, how he passed just as many challenges as she did. "If he had been my brother growing up, I would have forced him to work for…" she broke off as she realized what she had said.

"I didn't think." She felt her cheeks redden. "Here I am, complaining about that waste of space, when we should be concentrating on where Delphorus went."

The stream came into view in front of them.

"Yes, well, he could not have traveled much farther on his own." Origon finally said.

"Whatever he found must have been a few days walk or less," Rilan agreed. She pressed a hand to the side of her chest. The hike this morning had taken more out of her than she liked. "He was close to death when he fell near the edge of the forest.

He wouldn't have traveled far like that." She glanced to Origon. "Sorry."

He nodded, bent, and filled his canteen. Rilan did likewise.

"Give yours to me," he said. When she did, he took the caps off and held both, an orange aura springing up around his hands and the containers. Steam rose for a moment from the open caps, then disappeared. When he gave her back her canteen, the water was just as cool as the flowing stream.

"There were small creatures in the water that would be causing sickness," he said. "Now there are not."

Rilan took her canteen back. She would have known that, if she thought about it. But Origon had much more experience traveling through the wilderness. If she had somehow changed the creatures so they were not toxic, it would have taken a permanent investment from her, and she would have lost those notes of her song. It would have taken a few days to build them back up. But Origon merely applied heat, then took the heat back—a reversible change. The houses of the maji had many ways to accomplish the same goals, but some were better than others.

She took a sip of water, grunting, as raising her arm pulled on her rib. Clean and clear. "Can you tell which way your brother came from?"

"Last night, the air remembered him passing this direction," he said, gesturing with a long finger past the stream.

"But I cannot be forming another map to trace him from here. The connections are too sporadic."

"Then we continue in that direction until we find another clue." Rilan pulled a strip of jerky out of her bag and began to chew it, moistening the meat with water from her canteen. If there were any berries or nuts in the woods she would have eaten those instead, after using the House of Healing to make sure they weren't toxic. But it didn't seem to be the season for fruit, if the scrubby bushes even fruited here. She wasn't sure what season it was locally, though the air was hot.

Origon limped along behind her, occasionally reaching out with one finger, smoking in the humid morning air and ringed with an orange aura.

"What are you doing?"

"Breakfast." As he answered, Origon reached out and Rilan saw a large beetle fall out of the air—faster than she expected—crisping from the heat coming off the Kirian's finger. He caught it with his other hand and popped it in his mouth.

Rilan shook her head, then stopped when it hurt too much. "One of these days, you're going to catch a disease from eating foreign bugs."

Origon only smiled, chewing. "The heat is sterilizing the insects, just as it did the water." He caught another delicate flying thing with the finger and it fell from the air, smoking. "Even if they are to be overcooked."

Rilan opened her mouth to argue, but an odd shape on the ground ahead caught her eye. "What's that?"

She moved to the shape, holding her chest, then called Origon over.

"It's the ones from last night," she said. In front of them were two large carcasses, insects already buzzing around. The sharp metallic smell was strong, but mixed with others now; blood, and effluent, and death.

"Are you sure?" Origon toasted one of the flies that got too close to him.

"Positive. I copied their pheromones. I can tell these are the same. Besides, these are apex predators. There wouldn't be others so close."

"It is like they were tearing each other to pieces." Origon gingerly poked at a strip of flesh hanging from the nearest beast. In the daylight, they looked like a cross between the jaguars that frequented the jungles near Rilan's home city of Dalhni and some sort of hulking, hairy bear. They had long hooked claws to allow them to catch branches of the bare trees around them. She didn't look closely at the mouth. She had seen quite enough of that the night before.

"Which pheromones were you using?" Origon asked the question casually, but she caught him glancing at her.

It looked like the beasts had died from the deep clawed wounds. There was a trail of guts from one of the beasts.

"Unless they like to kill each other while mating, I don't think I caused this."

"Then why are they dead?"

Rilan looked closer. There were more wounds on the creature's backs, but these were half-closed, and scabbed over. "Something isn't right. Look here." She pointed to a long slash of purple down one of the beasts' backs. She listened for the Symphony.

The music was slowing, becoming lethargic. They hadn't been dead long, but there was another melody underneath, something running counter to the creature's natural tendencies.

"Someone changed them," she said. "And not very well."

"The majus?" Origon's crest rose with interest.

"It must be, but not a very good one."

"It is to be one of the House of Healing, then."

"Ye-es," Rilan hedged. "There was a component of my house involved, but there was something else, too. I can't hear what it is."

"So our majus might be a member of two houses, as I am."

"Isn't that rare?" Rilan looked at Origon. "An order of magnitude higher than those born able to hear one Symphony? You're the only one I know of."

Origon shrugged. She knew he was trying to look humble. He wasn't succeeding. "You know others. We are tending not to advertise our other abilities, rare though we are."

"Still, they aren't common," Rilan said. "Why would a majus be in the middle of nowhere modifying wild animals?" She gestured at the nearest corpse. "Why don't you give a listen. Maybe you can hear other changes."

He looked surprised by her request, only for a moment. "That is to be…a good idea."

"I do have them sometimes."

He bent over the beasts, head cocked, crest fluttering. "I cannot hear any changes to the Symphony."

"Then the other ability was the House of Strength, Grace, or Potential," Rilan concluded.

"Most likely Potential, to be able to store changes to the Symphony," Origon said.

"So what did this have to do with your brother?"

The Kirian's face fell, crest drooping. "I do not know." His large eyes met hers. "But I will be finding out."

A shiver ran down her back at his expression.

"Are there enough clues here to determine where they came from before they attacked us?" Rilan could potentially trace their biological footprint, but she wanted to give Origon something to focus on with the House of Power.

"I will try." As he moved again to the bodies, a deep grunt rang through the forest. Rilan jerked her head and bit back a curse at the pain. She felt her braid hit her shoulder, the little bell at the end chiming.

"Origon."

"I am seeing it." Origon rose, very slowly, his robe clinging around his legs. Another beast stood not twenty paces away, a deep rumbling coming from it. It was either purring or growling, and Rilan didn't want to find out which.

It roared, and its two tiers of serrated teeth shone between its tusks.

"No more apex predators?" Origon asked.

"So maybe we were near the edge of their territory," Rilan snapped, looking for anything to use against the thing. Aside from dead branches, there was nothing. She scooped one up, holding it in both hands. It wouldn't do much, but might give her enough time to make contact with it without losing an arm. Or her face.

It charged.

Origon's skinny arms rotated forward like he was trying to flourish a handkerchief toward the creature.

"Exhale!" he shouted, and Rilan felt the air pressure drop around her, like a storm was approaching. She blew out the air in her lungs. Her rib screamed at her.

There was a deep *thump* and her ears popped. The beast skidded to a stop, shaking its great head as if confused. She saw a trickle of bright purple blood flow from one large ear, and then from the gash of a nose above its teeth. It gave an almost pitiful moan and flopped to its side.

"Is it dead?" Rilan edged closer to the mound of fur. There was something very wrong here.

"I am sincerely hoping so. I cannot be generating so big a change in air pressure for a long time, or unless we are far away from here."

"There can't be that many predators nearby, not this large. And I doubt we're on their regular diet, since we're not even from this homeworld." She stepped closer still. She didn't see any movement.

"You are right." She looked back. Origon was listening to something again. "There is to be some connection here, in tune with the structure of the ecosystem. I can almost tell—"

He was interrupted by another grunt, followed by a snarl.

Four more beasts moved out from behind trees, one far bigger than the others, with fur black as pitch. The others were in shades of gray and brown. With a *whump* of displaced shavings, a fifth dropped from the trees behind her and Origon. They were surrounded, the corpse of the beast Origon had killed blocking their only exit.

"Are you sure you can't make the pressure change again?" Rilan hoped her voice didn't shake. The Symphony came to her, and she followed the unspoken pheromone exchange between the beasts:

Food.

Hungry.

Prey.

Origon cried out, and all the creatures turned toward him. Heedless, he limped in a run toward the one he had felled.

Rilan rotated in a circle, falling into the steps of *Fading Hands*, though it would do little good against this crowd. She wouldn't even be able to use her hands effectively with her broken rib. She began to pick apart the notes of the pheromones, hoping to create something to buy them more time.

"I have it!" Origon cried, holding up something that had been strapped to the creature's back. The rest watched him, heads tilting, their motion stopped for the moment by confusion or interest.

Then their heads snapped back to her, almost in unison. She felt their stares boring into her.

"They are all connected!" Origon called, and twisted the thing in his hands, arms held above his head like a madman. Rilan could only spare a small section of her attention to what he was doing.

There was a snap like wood splitting and the pheromones in the air suddenly changed. The beasts looked at each other, grunting and calling. Then one turned and stalked away.

Another caught a tree and pulled itself into the branches. Two more traded cuffs, knocking each other's heads with their wicked claws, then scampered away, catching branches at a distance.

The last, the great black-furred one, circled her. She could hear it snorting and sniffing. The three tusks pointed toward her, away, toward her again…and then it turned with a *whuff* of air, kicking shavings back toward her as if she wasn't worth the effort.

It wandered off.

Rilan let out a breath she didn't know she had been holding, her arms slowly drooping from her guard position. Her legs were nearly locked into a stance of *Fading Hands*. It would have done no good with her muscles so tight. Her ribs complained at the movement, as her adrenaline rush faded.

"This is the key!" Origon called, gesturing with something. Rilan stalked toward him, fists clenched.

"What was that? Are you insane? We could have been killed and you just run off like you're chasing butterflies!"

Origon fell back, his crest flattening at her admonishment. He held the pieces of something out in both hands as if it explained his actions.

"What. What is it?" Rilan gestured impatiently for him to hand over the objects. He did, with a look of trepidation.

It once was a medallion made of wood, with lines carved into it in a now unreadable pattern. Origon had shattered it into five uneven pieces, each of which held the fading orange and brown auras of two of the houses.

"You heard the change from the House of Power." It wasn't a question.

Origon nodded. "That was the connection I was hearing. It became louder as more of the creatures came closer. They are solitary, but their hierarchy was adjusted with my house so they were becoming a pack, tracking intruders. I am believing each of them has one of these."

"Why did breaking one medallion destroy the pack bond?" Rilan wasn't questioning their good fortune, but it did seem odd.

"The web of Power between them was very fine," Origon answered. He brushed his moustaches down, smoothing them. "Each one was to be connected to each other. The medallions might have been created together, though I cannot tell. The creation was using the House of Potential. Breaking one must have tangled enough strings of the web to be bringing the entire construct down. To rewrite a Symphony of such complexity and size would use many notes of one's song. There are many parts I cannot hear, or I would be knowing more."

Rilan lifted one of the pieces. She could barely make out discordant notes, fading rapidly. "My house was used in the medallion too. It adjusted their behavior so they could live together for long periods of time. I must have disrupted that when I increased the mated pair's sex drive."

Origon nodded. "It is quite ingenious. Despite the change in the House of Healing being sloppy, the overall change was to be well crafted."

Rilan frowned as she tucked the broken pieces of what had been an artifact into her vest pocket. Something still didn't add up. "Three houses, and used in a harmony and precision that rivals some of the Council's workings. Are there two maji?"

Now Origon frowned. "You are correct. Even if one majus was of two houses, that person would have had help to craft this."

"You've never heard of someone belonging to three houses, have you?" Rilan asked. It was a silly question. Everyone knew the answer.

But Origon took it seriously, pacing through shavings on the forest floor. "There are schools of thought among the houses—especially with those who are members of more than one—postulating why there are to be maji who can hear two Symphonies. There has never been any recorded case where a majus has heard more than two. The prevailing thought is to be that the strain on the mind is too great. Those who would hear more than two aspects of the Grand Symphony die before they are born."

Visions of secret societies and meetings in the dark flitted through Rilan's imagination. She was only beginning her path to become a majus, and there were still many secrets to unlock in the houses. She looked at her friend, her lover, her old teacher in a new light. How long had he been steeped in that even more rarified atmosphere?

"Can you determine who has touched it?" he asked, breaking through her reverie. His face was questioning; no hint of any secrets.

"Touched…what?" Rilan shook her head, carefully, to keep her rib from taking offense at the action. "Oh, the artifact." She drew one of the larger pieces out of her pocket, hearing the topmost layer of the Symphony even as she did. She banished the thought of secret societies to the back of her mind, assigning a mnemonic to it so she wouldn't forget.

The overwhelming sense of the broken medallion was of the beast to which it had been attached. Muscles bunching and loosening, prey caught, and several wild sprints through the branches.

It had only been attached for two days, and she could still feel the residue of the one who had created it.

The *one*.

She frowned. "This has only been touched by one majus."

Origon's crest fluttered in alarm and he stopped pacing. "Are you sure?"

"I think…yes, though there is interference behind it. But only one majus put notes of their song into this medallion— permanently." Doing so would make the change to the Symphony last much longer, but would weaken the majus for days afterward.

"Are we to be speaking of a majus with access to more than two Symphonies?"

"I'll only believe it if I see it," Rilan answered.

"How are we to be finding them?" Origon looked around as if one might just pop out of the scenery.

Rilan thought for a moment. There was plenty of data here, between the remains of the beast, the medallion, and the change in the group structure of the beasts. But they would need to work together.

"I think we can take a page from our mystery majus' book," she said. "Can you find the connections between the group of beasts that ambushed us? I can add a biological tracker with my house."

Origon thumbed his wispy moustache for a moment, then listened to something hidden from her. "I am having a better idea." He gestured to the air with one hand, as if pulling ropes, and lines of yellow formed, twisting paths following where the beasts had been. Rilan watched him work. He was doing something with the House of Communication, tracking the air currents and communication between the animals. It took time to identify the correct chords of the Symphony. If they were too fast or too strong, it would be harder to change, more prone to failure. But Origon was quick, and decisive. His other hand came forward and orange light flashed between the yellow ropes, lightning strikes of the interchanges of power and hierarchy between the group. He began to walk forward, favoring his good leg, not even looking to see if Rilan was behind him.

"Or you could do it yourself," Rilan mumbled. "So the maji of the Great Assembly work for the good of all…"

She followed Origon, one hand on her aching rib.

HIDDEN CHORDS

- Upon answering the Lobath's summons, I found his mate near death in childbirth with severe complications. After a lengthy procedure, I saved the female Lobath's life. The child, however was stillborn and disfigured in strange ways, as if its body skipped some stages of growth and accelerated others. Medically, I cannot say what happened. One of my colleagues in the House of Healing believes the infant was actively changing three of the six Symphonies. This is, of course, impossible. Nevertheless, the House of Healing followed the woman's progress for several cycles until she birthed two completely healthy, and otherwise unremarkable, children.

Fragment of a medical diagnosis found in the archives of the House of Healing, 506 AAW

The land rose steadily until they found the entrance to the cave. It was set amidst a cluster of giant cilia-bark trees, and if Origon's ropes of yellow and orange hadn't pointed directly to the entrance, Rilan would have missed it.

The entrance was low, but soon opened up into a larger cavern, tall enough even for Origon to stand straight. Rilan was thankful for that, as bending didn't help her rib any. The walls were natural, a crack in the crust of the earth. Small animals had made their mark here and there. She wondered if the sabretooth beasts used this cave too.

"Look." She pointed toward a covered lantern hanging from a hook in the wall. An orange aura surrounded it, but it gave physical light as well—a soft yellow glow. Rilan knew it would give that light for many cycles, notes from the House of Power stored by one of the House of Potential. They were common in the Nether. Not so much in the wilds of Festuour.

"This is to be the correct location." Origon made a dismissive motion. The yellow and orange ropes around them vanished as he sucked in a long breath, his music returning to him, the changes to the Symphony reversed. He limped forward, and Rilan followed him with a grunt. Either standing or walking was fine, but her rib didn't like changing between the two.

They followed the chain of lights, set in crevices in the walls. The rough floor descended steadily down, while the roof soared far overhead. In places where the walls would be too narrow to pass through, there were marks of tools, expanding the passage.

"There are to be many lights," Origon remarked. At first Rilan wondered what he meant, but then she saw. The majus lights were set at regular intervals, no more than a few paces apart. Each had their faint aura of orange, with hints of brown to show the work of one of the House of Potential, though the aura gave no real light. They lit the passage very well. Too well. There was more than enough to keep good footing along the passage.

"Why would a majus expend so much of their song on a permanent investment?" Rilan asked. Origon nodded in agreement.

"It is as if this majus does not understand the costs of making permanent changes to the Symphony." Before long, the majus would become weak, unable to craft the larger changes more complicated works required.

They followed the passage until the first pipes began to appear.

"What are those?" Rilan whispered as she pointed to a brace holding two long cylinders, one of a thin beaten metal, and the other of what looked to be stiff oiled fabric. Their voices dropped in volume the farther they went.

"Vents?" Origon offered. "Maybe there is to be no good source of air deep in the cavern."

"Hmm." Rilan watched another pipe emerge from above and join the other two as they walked. "Or maybe there is something below generating fumes that need ventilation." She sniffed, but the air was still fresh, if a little musty.

"Perhaps we should be moving more quietly," Origon suggested. The cave was alive with little noises; drips, creaks, and rustlings. It covered the sounds of a person moving slowly and carefully. Still, best to be safe.

"I don't think I'm the problem." She glanced down at Origon's thick boots, just peeping from underneath the edge of his now filthy robe hem. He was clumping along louder than usual, with his limp, but he made an effort to reduce his noise. She tried to silence the sound of her labored breathing.

The cavern passage split several times, but always the lights went one direction, and they followed. More pipes joined the three, until there was a bundle on each side, above their heads. There was more metal now, though a few pipes were still made of oiled fabric. Rilan could see valves, gears, and pressure catches in the light from the lamps. Origon was paying careful attention to them, and she wondered if he was listening to the Symphony of Power. What would it tell him about the forces directed along the pipes?

Before long, another sound began to intrude on the other ambient noises. It was continuous, a hissing tick every few seconds like a large clock run by steam. Rilan traded glances with Origon. There was a brighter glow ahead, where the passage took a turn to the left.

"Someone has been here a long time," Origon whispered.

Rilan positioned herself just before the turn in the corridor, gesturing Origon beside her. The rough wall poked her back. She could see marks around the bright entrance, as if someone made an effort to make the opening regular.

She held up three fingers, then two, then—

Origon silently turned into the room ahead of her. Rilan rolled her eyes and followed him, her cracked rib complaining at resuming movement.

The room was illuminated by many majus lights, and Rilan shielded her eyes until they adjusted. The run of pipes in the corridor had nothing on this room. Bunches of them reduced to smaller, thicker tubes, feeding into cabinets filled with whirring gears, pistons, and bellows. Dials and readouts fluctuated above them. Machinery lined the walls of the cavern, twenty or thirty paces across. Some of the equipment was mechanical, while other tables held chemical reagents. A large cabinet near the far wall was the source of the hiss-tick they heard in the hallway. Puffs of steam left it with every beat, and dials spun in the body of the thing. In the middle of the room was a table, obscured by the furry figure bent over it. It was a Festuour.

Origon was in the middle of the doorway, Rilan positioned behind him. They hadn't been seen, and she was just about to pull Origon back when the figure turned.

"Oh! You're early." The Festuour—Rilan was pretty sure it was female, and somehow familiar, at that—was draped in an apron filled with pockets holding calipers, pencils, rulers, and scientific looking devices for which she had no name. The Festuour glanced at a dial on the wall through three pairs of spectacles set at various distances down her snout. "I was sure as punch you would get here twenty minutes later. No matter."

She drew one of the devices from her apron—a tube with a piston on one end and a dial on the other. She waved it in Rilan's direction and it made a whistling noise, creating a strange harmonic with the Symphony. Rilan shook her head. "House of Healing. Fine." The Festuour waved her device at Origon and Rilan saw his crest flare. He swayed back in surprise. "And House of Power. Have one of those already." She lifted the middle pair of spectacles and peered through the other two, then turned the dial on the side of the device. "And the House of Communication! That's much better."

Rilan tensed.

"I don't have many visitors out here, as you must imagine," the Festuour told them. Her voice was high, her fur brown and green in patches. She was not old, from what Rilan could tell. Was this their fearsome adversary?

"And so many these last few days!" the Festuour continued. "Well, you must admit, that's surprising as can be. Still, I try to be a hospitable host."

Rilan looked at Origon again. More visitors.

"Someone else has been here? Another Kirian?" she asked. The Festuour blinked at her, seeming not to hear.

"You must excuse my manners. Let me introduce myself. I am Aptibontigon Ket, Maker. Fernand Vethis has told me much about you."

"Wait. *Vethis?*" Rilan wondered if she heard wrong, then realized why the Festuour looked familiar. It was the one she had seen him with after their test.

Ket moved her mass to one side. "Yes. Didn't he tell you he was coming? Let me guess. Wanted to keep all the fun for himself." The Festuour was certainly a majus. They had no trouble communicating, and Rilan was making no effort to translate her words.

There was a body on the table Ket had been leaning over. Rilan saw enough of the dark hair and a hint of his face to recognize her classmate. What had he gotten into now, and how? Was he even still alive?

"What about my brother?" Origon's hands were at his side, clenched. His crest rose like a fan. He spoke before she could ask more about her rival classmate, motionless on the table.

Ket blinked again. "I'm afraid I don't know anything about him. You must explain. What house does he belong to?"

"He is not a majus."

Ket pulled her middle set of spectacles off again. Glancing down at the strange instrument she still held, she fiddled with it, then pointed it at Origon. "Curious. You are older than he, I gather." She seemed unconcerned they had found her.

Apprentice Fernand Vethis

"I…" Origon stopped short, his hands loosening. "I am. How are you knowing that?" Rilan took advantage of their conversation to sidle slightly to one side. Maybe she could get close enough to see what Ket had done to Vethis. If he was here now, he must have left around the same time they did. She *had* seen them again the morning they left. Ket could have brought him directly here, of course, but why? What did he have to do with this?

"You belong to two houses," Ket said, as if it were self-explanatory. Then she made an annoyed click of her tongue. "I forget others haven't studied the theory of the Grand Symphony as much as I have. I studied acoustics when I was young, you know. Still do."

Rilan concentrated on getting out of the Festuour's field of view, using slow footwork from *Fading Hands*, though the creature was as good as ignoring her. Maybe it would have been better to go on the offensive immediately and incapacitate the majus, but something in her protested against such violence when their opponent was so calm. And, her rib hurt too much.

"I have studied several maji belonging to two houses. In all cases, their birth was followed soon after by a younger brother or sister, devoid of any talent with the Symphony." Ket spoke earnestly to Origon, as if delivering a thesis to the Council.

"This is not to be unusual," Origon countered. "Many maji have siblings. The ability is rare enough that it often does not show in families." Rilan would have laughed if she wasn't so tense. Just like a Kirian to start debating a point when faced with a potentially lethal adversary in a hidden underground lab.

"Yes, but in these cases, the sibling was usually sickly, did not make much of themselves, and often perished young."

Rilan could see Origon's face tighten. She was almost around the room now, and had a better view of the table. It was definitely Vethis, and he was merely unconscious, not dead. He had some sort of fabric mask over his mouth, and a tube was inserted beneath the skin of his left wrist. That triggered another memory. Something about circular marks.

"It is my theory," Ket continued, "That the elder sibling sometimes takes the potential that would be passed on to the second child. The older one robs the younger one, if you will, of its future as a majus." Her voice was easy and calm, as if speaking over a casual lunch.

When Origon started forward, Rilan took the chance to move closer to the table, tracing the tube under Vethis' wrist. "I did not rob my brother! I was caring for him, his whole life." His voice rose, his hands trembling as they reached forward. "I was going to visit him again soon, before I was getting the message—"

"Yes, and you see what happened to him," Ket interrupted. "Maybe if he had access to that second house you wield, he would have lived. Maybe he could have fended off the thrycovolars that followed him. They don't usually hunt people, whatever species."

"You—!" Origon's normally pale skin was growing more flushed by the moment. Rilan glanced between them. The Festuour knew about Delphorus. She had killed him, or let him be killed.

But Delphorus hadn't had any marks on him. She remembered the strips of flesh ripped off the beasts—the thrycovolars. They wouldn't have been able to recognize Origon's brother if the creatures had killed him. She watched Ket through narrowed eyes. What was the Festuour doing?

Origon had both hands up, a yellow and orange glow mixing around them. He was going to do something, and though the heads of the houses forbade maji to fight each other, Rilan wasn't sure she wanted to stop him. She traced where the other end of Vethis' tube vanished into a machine and guessed at the most likely off switch, stabbing down at a carved rocker. The Festuour was ignoring her, for whatever reason, focusing only on Origon. She could use that time to her advantage.

"It is truly a shame about your brother," Ket remarked, hurrying to the hissing machine on the other side of the room. She switched topics. "You must tell me how the mixture of the Houses of Communication and Power changes the way the Symphony is heard." She twisted dials and flipped knobs, glancing back at Origon every few moments.

Rilan's machine sighed, and some life went out of it. She went back to Vethis, sparing a glance at Origon, who was having some difficulty, the aura around him pulsing and fading. The change he was preparing must be particularly complex.

"I'll need that information after all," Ket said, "when I get used to the new house."

Connections bloomed in Rilan's mind. Ket *wanted* Origon to attack her. She reached a hand out, wincing at the ache. "Ori—"

Something beeped near Vethis and Ket spun. "Oh, you mustn't do that." She gestured, and a brown aura flashed across the room. The House of Potential. The machine behind Rilan started back up. Rilan watched with wide eyes. To rewrite the Symphony of a complex machine was a difficult thing, nearly as hard as rewriting the Symphony of a living thing. And the Festuour had done it at a distance without hesitation. Rilan would have needed several moments to catch the measure and tone of a person's music. Ket was fast, and powerful.

Then she saw Origon, slowly sinking to the floor. She was too late. The orange haze was still around him, but the yellow one was gone, or very faint. Across the room, another yellow aura hovered near the hiss-tick machine by Ket. She had transferred it somehow; stolen the change he made to the Symphony. Origon would lose those notes of his song. No wonder he had buckled.

Rilan pressed the rocker switch again. Anything Ket didn't want her to do was a good thing. When the beep sounded once more, the rogue majus was buried in the dials and didn't seem to hear it. Rilan patted at Vethis' cheek, while keeping an eye on Origon. The Kirian was pale and gasping, but still conscious.

"Wake up!" she hissed. Any ally would be an asset, even an arrogant fop like Vethis. He murmured something and his eyelids fluttered. Origon was on his knees, and Ket was still at the controls, doing something. Rilan made eye contact with her friend and made a motion toward him. He shook his head, very slightly, and gestured her back to the table. He wanted her to wake Vethis up too.

Gently, Rilan pulled the tube back out of Vethis' wrist. It wasn't in deep, but the diameter narrowed to a point. It was probably injecting some concoction straight into his veins. She only just had it out, blotting the small wound, when Ket turned back, taking in the whole situation with one look.

She tsked. "Really now, that's rude of you. Do you know how long it took me to prep him? I only perfected the technique a ten-day ago, and I haven't had the chance to complete the transfer." The Festuour pushed out with both hands and something glowed between them, both giving off real orange light and ringed with the orange of the House of Power.

Her second house. She had already demonstrated the House of Potential. Rilan had no idea what the majus was capable of. She began to time the beat of her own song, getting ready.

As Ket pushed outward, the ring of orange expanded forward, leaving her fingers and moving toward Rilan. She guessed the majus was manipulating heat and changed notes to toughen her skin. Her eyes flicked to Vethis. She didn't have time to change his melody too.

Origon, from his knees, curved his fingers through an arc in the air, then slumped again. The wave of orange bowed away from her, toward the high ceiling of the cavern.

Rilan felt an intense drying heat frizzle her hair and shivered involuntarily. Her change would not have stopped that. She quickly reversed what she had done, regaining that part of her song. She would need it.

Ket snapped her long jaws together—a sign of irritation in Festuour—and began some other change in the Symphony of Power. Too late she realized what Rilan saw. Origon hadn't just deflected the wave of heat, he had taken the change from her—a permanent investment on his part. Her friend had a hand on the floor, holding himself up. Oddly, Ket didn't seem to notice. Rilan winced at his loss, even as the orange wave curved back down.

Ket followed Rilan's involuntary glance upward and the haze around her graduated from orange to a brilliant white in a split second. Rilan heard chords change, almost quicker than she could register. Origon's eyes widened. The wave of heat washed over Ket and her fur crinkled, but there was no other effect. The brilliant white faded.

The Festuour had switched Symphonies, mid-tune. To her *third* house.

"I have few notes of that kind of song left to waste," Ket said. "Either of you two can provide me with more." She gestured beside Rilan. Vethis had his eyes open, and was pulling the mask from his face.

"She has a machine that steals a majus' song," Vethis said, his voice hoarse, his clipped, affected accent barely showing through. "She stole those notes from me. And she stole something from that other Kirian."

"Is that even possible?" Rilan asked.

Vethis glared up at her. "I thought you were supposed to be the smart one." His accent was already clearer.

"Of course it is," Ket put in. "I had experimented on Kiria with the energy transfer before I was…interrupted." She looked annoyed.

Origon regained his feet, shaking his head as if clearing it. He growled something, and his crest looked like he had been struck by lightning. Rilan helped Vethis sit up, gathering her song and planning how best to disable Ket. She only needed a moment to—

"You must excuse me. I'm afraid I won't be a very good host to three maji." Ket walked, fast, to the only other blank section of wall. There was a medallion hanging on it, like the ones they had seen on the creatures outside. They must have been artifacts of the House of Potential— storing larger systems of changes to the Symphony.

"My brother!" Origon rushed forward at the same time as Rilan. The room wasn't big, but Ket moved faster. A bright aura erupted from her, brown and orange and white all together. The yellow aura around the hiss-tick machine flew to her and joined the mix. The medallion flashed in response, glowing incandescent. Just as Rilan got to the Festuour, gritting her teeth against the pain in her chest, the wall in front of her dissolved into nothingness and Ket scooted through.

Rilan skidded to a stop as the wall re-solidified in front of her nose. She fell against the hard surface as Origon bumped into her from behind. She made a pained sound, one hand going to her ribs.

"What was that?" he said over her shoulder. He reached out a long finger and scraped down the wall. It was hard as stone. There was no way they could burrow through in time.

Rilan could only shake her head. "I have no idea. Solidified air and fire, made organic? Pure kinetic energy converted to solid matter? With four houses mixed together, the possibilities are endless. Ket must have heard almost the entire Grand Symphony underlying the universe, all at once. It's enough to make anyone mad." Ket was definitely not operating on the same tune as the rest of them.

She turned around as Origon backed away. Vethis was shakily getting to his feet, one hand already preening his hair. "We can't relax," she said. "No telling when she'll come back. We must keep watch." Rilan frowned, looking around the cavern, trying to think of a way to get to the majus.

"I think she was using up most of the notes she stole from me. Luckily, she was not taking all of them. She could be limited to only three houses now." As he spoke, Origon stepped toward the medallion, eyeing it while one hand stroked his moustaches meditatively.

"Or two," Vethis added. "She might not have much left from the House of Healing after what she put into those horrible beasts." His affected accent was back full force—something popular with the other aristocratic prats where he hailed from, some city far to the north of Rilan's birth town.

Rilan crossed to the apprentice. He shouldn't even be out of the Nether before he tested. She wondered when she had started taking for granted that she was a majus. "Speaking of which, what, by Shiv's labyrinthine guts, are *you* doing here?"

Vethis flinched back, raising a velvet sleeve. He was still dressed in the clothes from their test, black-blue velvet coat, striped pants, and white cuffs. A deep blue collar—his secondary color—set off his dark hair.

"I might ask you the same," he returned, peering down his thin nose at her. "Shouldn't you be doing some great deed with the rest of the maji, now you're one of them? Too good for the rest of us—the second best—eh?"

"Answer the question, *apprentice*," Origon said from behind her. "How were you getting here ahead of us? What were you seeing of my brother? Are you knowing where Ket went?"

"I can't tell you much." Vethis sniffed. "The other Kirian was already dead when I got here. That wretched pretend majus drained the life right out of him. It was a terrible experiment on her part. She said something about paying him back for interrupting her." He closed his mouth, eyeing them. When Origon's crest flared and he limped forward, Vethis backed up and began speaking again.

"As to how I got here, the despicable creature invited me. First she wanted information. She picked the right person to come to, of course." Rilan rolled her eyes and motioned for him to continue. "The strange thing was, she wanted information on *him*." Vethis pointed at Origon. "Of course, now I know she wanted him because of his brother. At the time, I thought she had some other purpose, so I was very willing to share what I knew of *you two*." He grinned at her and she wondered how much of the Nether was talking about her and Origon. Then Vethis frowned. "But she wasn't interested in what I had to offer. She started on about a new source of power for all maji, so I went with her. I had no clue the source would be *me*." Origon turned away from Vethis, his wrinkled face twisting in a grimace.

Of course her classmate jumped at that chance. Any whisper of power or influence and he was on it like a Kirian on a grub. He must have been an easy target for the rogue majus, especially after failing his test. Another thought struck her. Ket had been *at* their test. If Rilan had been the one to fail, would Ket have come after her instead? Of course she wouldn't have taken the bait. That feeling of dread when she thought she might fail rose up within her. She hoped she wouldn't have taken it.

Origon grunted behind her and Rilan turned to him too quickly. The heaviness of this world made her rib feel like it was cracking all over again whenever she moved.

"I cannot hear a large enough part of the melody." He was fiddling with the medallion now, yellow and orange sparking between his fingers. "The music is to be too fast for me to catch, and there is too much of at least one other house in it." He shifted, and almost fell as his leg gave out under him.

"Oh for the sake of all that's holy," Vethis said. "Are you still that terrible with healing, Rilan? It's in the *name* of our house, you know."

Rilan glared at him, even as he reached for her. If he touched anything but her ribs, he was drawing back a nub.

But Vethis' fingers were strangely gentle, white and the dark blue of his personal color extending from his hands to the outline of her ribcage. Rilan couldn't quite make out what he did. The melody for encouraging pure healing was almost impossible for her to change, like trying to whistle a base drumbeat. Each majus had areas where they were more skilled.

"There. That should feel better." Vethis watched her until she gave a grudging nod, rotating an arm. It did feel better, but he wasn't getting out of this that easy. He gave her a knowing half-smile and went to Origon, who received Vethis' attentions with a grunt of thanks, still investigating the medallion.

"Don't thank me," Vethis responded, straightening his hair again. "Healing you two means I have a better chance of getting out alive. That crazy bear is tough."

"And she may be coming back at any point," Origon put in. "Do you know where she went? Why was she needing my stolen notes to create the door it if it was there previously?"

Vethis shook his head. "I didn't even know it *was* there. I've been on that table most of the last two days." He pointed with a limp finger toward the table in the middle of the room. "I suspect you're not going to let me make a portal back to the Nether and be done with this mess." Rilan glared at him. Origon's crest had gone all spiky again. "Didn't think so."

"We cannot be letting this criminal loose again," Origon said. "She has already killed several times."

"What is she doing in there?" Rilan smacked the wall with one palm where the doorway had been. It was hard, unyielding. Origon began to investigate each machine in turn.

Vethis watched them both, arms crossed. "Is she even in there any longer? She could have made a portal to anywhere by now. As *we* should."

Rilan ignored him, grasping her braid and pulling it around front. She tapped the bell into her palm with a tiny jingle. *Think.*

"Should we be destroying her equipment?" Origon asked from halfway across the room.

"We don't even know what it does," Rilan told him, watching his progress over one shoulder. "It could all be to vent chemicals to the outside, for what we know."

Vethis pointed at the hiss-tick machine. "That one steals the song from a majus. Or were you not paying attention again? I wonder how you even passed your test."

Origon shrugged and went for the machine, but Rilan waved him away. "And what happens if we beat it to pieces? Have you ever heard of any machine like that? It could suck the rest of our songs away if it malfunctions. We should be figuring out how to get to Ket."

"But what if the design is getting out?" Origon asked. "Imagine if more people could be arbitrarily stealing one's house and song."

Rilan almost missed the gleam in Vethis' eye. She stared him down, daring him to move toward the machine. "Maybe it is better to destroy it." She started to turn away from where Ket had disappeared.

At that moment the wall in front of her dissolved.

Ket snarled, flinging something glowing white, orange and brown at her. It was another medallion. It stuck to her chest, and a searing pain coursed through her. She stumbled back, gasping, hearing Origon yell something. All her senses were going black.

Then there was an intense white light. As Rilan fell back into the table, she saw her hand glowing. Was she changing the Symphony without knowing it? What was happening?

Origon was beside her as her eyes cleared and she saw the little bell in her hand, now devoid of any aura.

It will ward off disease. Thank you, Majus Meyta. Whatever the majus had thrown at her had some element of the House of Healing holding it together, and not a pleasant one.

For once, Ket looked surprised. "You should be dead," she complained, as she closed the distance between them.

"You're not actually very good, are you?" Rilan said, backpedaling. "Fast, yes, and you have lots of power. I would too if I stole it from others." She got back to her feet, Origon beside her. "Are you even a majus? I've never heard of you." Out of the corner of her eye she saw Vethis bolt for the secret room, getting away from the fight. *Coward.*

Ket looked uncertain for only a moment, then her long face twisted up. "I'll be the most powerful majus ever," she said. She started some change, orange and yellow flaring around her arms, but Origon stepped in front of Rilan, hands moving. The air rippled as a curve of compressed air came into being, like the tent when they camped.

Ket's changes beat against the shield, making it wobble. "You must be pleased. Your kind is so smug, controlling the Assembly and all the species. Just because someone is a majus, they're automatically at the top of their field." She flung a hand out, orange and brown ringing it, and it passed completely through Origon's shield. Rilan gasped, something burning in her chest, but only for a moment. Origon had both hands out, his head cocked like he was trying to get a note just right. His crest came to a point in concentration, then relaxed. The heat left her.

"The maji are to be providing for all species," he said. "If some are renowned for their jobs as well, it is because they worked hard to get there." He was brewing another change as he spoke, yellow and orange roiling around his hands. Yet he still kept the shield in place. It would take more concentration, but if he let it fall, he would not be able to make another one for a while. Rilan fell into her own Symphony, listening to all the music of life in the room. Ket's music was off, tempo jerking and stopping. Accessing that many houses was not good for her body. Rilan tried to find a way to incapacitate her.

"*I* worked hard," the Festuour said. "*I* should have been at the top of my field. Why should only maji study the Grand Symphony? It's a beautiful thing. Did you know there are ways to hear the notes mechanically? It's only science. But you maji don't quantify it—you don't study it. You *worship* it."

A glow surrounded Ket suddenly, appearing all at once. It was a large change to the Symphony, and made quickly. Rilan finally understood. Everything Ket did was a permanent change to the Symphony. She wasn't trying to regain any notes, so of course her changes were more powerful—she didn't have to be careful to make reversible changes, the way other maji did. And why not? Everything she was using was stolen. If she ran out, she could just steal more.

All this passed through Rilan's mind in a fraction of a second, while she watched Origon's hands rise slowly, starting to glow. He was making a change in both the House of Communication and Power, maybe another change to the air, maybe something else to defend against what was coming. Rilan began her own change, using her song to heighten her reactions. If she could get around Origon's shield in time to touch the Festuour, she could start destroying muscle and tissue. It wasn't pleasant, but it was quick. Entropy always was.

Though her senses processed faster, the Symphony was unchanged. It still played at its own pace, and she struggled to gather together all the phrases she would change to affect her opponent. She watched Ket's aura, orange and brown, spear toward her and too late to stop it, felt her contact with the Symphony falter. Her opponent was using the Houses of

Power and Potential in combination to sap Rilan's connection with the Symphony. This must be what Origon felt before.

Indeed, his yellow and orange construction was flickering too. Rilan saw bits of her own white and olive floating away from her, crossing the room to that terrible hiss-tick machine. She poured more concentration into her change but the notes slipped away, like the music was in another room, and then in another building. Her enhanced senses were slipping away too, the change stolen from her. The very notes making her song were leaving.

Rilan's knees buckled, and she saw Origon slump.

Then there was a hollow sound, like a melon being slapped, and Ket's blue eyes rolled back in their sockets. The suction stopped and Rilan stood, weakly.

Ket fell back to reveal Vethis, a hollow metal pipe dangling from his hands. He dropped it with a clang.

"Never liked the idea of fighting with the Symphony," he said, brushing his hands off with distaste. "It feels so crass."

RE-TUNING

- 4th of the Protector's Month, 979 AAW

Waveform function experiments performing well. I have determined there is a certain progression of chords in the Grand Symphony which may characterize one house of the magi from another.

- 32nd of the Protector's Month, 979 AAW

The House of Strength seems to exhibit the lowest notes of the Grand Symphony, often dipping below the lower threshold of my instruments. Made note to create a second set of connections in the resonancy chamber.

- 16th of the Watcher's Month, 979 AAW

The House of Healing is a very delicate Symphony compared to those of the other houses. Might be able to use harmonics to create a set of defining patterns. Similar to House of Potential in some aspects?

From the journal of Aptibontigon Ket, Maker.

"The room back there is absolutely filled with equipment," Vethis said. "I ducked in to see what I could find. There are a fair number of those blasted medallions, for one thing. And journals of notes, and lots of spare parts. I'm certain it takes an effort to keep these things running." Vethis gestured vaguely to the humming machinery.

Rilan stood erect, then pressed her hands against her legs to stop them shaking. She felt weak, drained.

"Thank you." It was one of the hardest things she had ever said. Vethis gave a tiny bow, smirking.

Origon had his hands on his knees, his purple and orange checked robe bunching around his skinny legs. "What shall we be doing with her?"

"We'll take her back to the Council, of course," Rilan said.

Vethis looked between both of them, one hand on his chin. "There are...other... things we can do, you know. No one need ever hear of this."

Rilan shook her head. "Absolutely not." She would have to be a whole lot weaker before she let Vethis get away with something like that.

Once she got her breath back, she leaned over the fallen Festuour, listening to the Symphony of Healing play out. She touched Ket's brow with one finger, sparking white and olive as she picked the right notes and changed them so the false majus would sleep. She didn't have to do much with the head injury. There was blood in her fur where Vethis hit her, still flowing. Rilan could tell from the Symphony it wouldn't kill her, but Ket would be out for a while.

She stood back up, wincing as pain spiked through her own head. "Let's see this room." She gestured Vethis forward, who led with a frown. She knew what he wanted, and he wasn't getting it if she got her way. Origon followed behind them.

The journals were the largest part of Ket's collection. They dated back nearly fifteen cycles. They spent some time looking through them, during which she and Origon both kept an eye on Vethis.

"Look here." Rilan waved a sheet. They had been reading for several minutes. "She was working with a majus from the House of Potential." She read the journal entry again. "One I don't recognize. Sounds like he had a heart attack and…the equipment somehow transferred his ability to her. She doesn't even know how it happened. I was right. She wasn't a majus, to begin with. Can that even happen?"

"I have never heard of it," Origon answered. "If it is possible, it would be shaking the maji to the very core. Our entire institution is depending on the scarcity of maji. Imagine if everyone could be changing the Symphony." Rilan saw Vethis give a dramatic shiver.

"What would that many changes to the Symphony do?"

"Most likely unravel the universe," Vethis said. He hefted a sheaf of notes. "But I believe the ability can only be stolen, or given away. She believed there was a natural constant to the maximum number of maji, a universal constant, if you will."

"She was beginning as merely an acoustic scientist," Origon added, reading his own pages. "She was to be working on a way to channel the Grand Symphony." He gestured to another page. "This is to be from three cycles ago. Are you remembering the majus north of Martflen that the sheriff mentioned?" Rilan nodded, recalling the Festuour's words, a chill running through her. He hadn't seen her for three cycles.

"That was to be her second victim," Origon said. "A majus of the House of Power. It was at the same time she made this lab." His face tightened, his crest hanging limply. "And then she began testing the apparatus on Kirians. Probably to keep the focus away from this location. Delphorus found out about her and began investigating. I believe he was merely in the wrong place at the wrong time, doing his duty. I am wondering if she even received any benefit from draining his energy away." He paused, as if unwilling to say his next words. "Maybe I was doing that long ago."

"You can't believe that," Rilan told him. "You can hear two of the six Symphonies that make up the universe. You didn't steal them. *She* did."

Origon nodded, but she could tell his heart wasn't in it. This would take a long time to heal, but it would, with her help.

Vethis didn't seem interested in the journals any longer, putting down his papers to poke through the spare parts. Pouting, more likely. He would have been the next victim. Ket must have only drained enough of his song to create the system making the beasts into her guard dogs. Why had she waited so long in between the majus north of Martflen and Vethis? Training her new powers, maybe, and building her equipment. It might explain why those changes were so well put together while the one from the House of Healing was so sloppy.

"How did she handle so many houses at once?" Rilan asked, both to change the subject, and out of curiosity. She hadn't found anything to explain that yet.

To her surprise, Vethis answered. "It's something that horrible machine does," he said, fingering a steam valve. "She created it. It lets the recipient keep from losing his or her mind, as well as stealing notes from maji. Otherwise she would have been dead by now." He looked up suddenly. "She, ah, mentioned something about it while I was lying on that table."

They finished looking through the notes, and took them back to the main room. They would take them to the Council along with Ket. This was too important to leave to any one majus.

Origon dusted his hands. "Are we ready to be going? I will open a portal from here and you can be taking the rogue majus through."

Of course he would give her the dirty work. "Come over here and help me," she called to Vethis. She wasn't picking up Ket all on her own. Festuour weren't light.

"One moment." Vethis' voice was airy, distracted. "Just one more thing."

Rilan heard the faint click at the same time as Origon. Both of them spun to the other side of the room, where Vethis was quietly adjusting dials on the hiss-tick machine.

"No!" Rilan reached out a hand, but it was too late. Something was already rising from Ket—a blob of orange and brown. She ran to the Festuour, but before she could gain the full score of the other's music, Ket had breathed her last.

"She deserved that," Vethis spat. "No one steals from me." He spun back to the machine, pulling levers and pushing buttons. "Now let's see how far behind I am, with three houses at my disposal. Give me only a few moments. I'll even be fair. You can try it after I do." How had he learned to use the machine? She knew the man wasn't stupid, just lazy. He must have observed Ket or seen instructions when he was in the secret room alone.

"Vethis, stop this!" Rilan shouted.

"No chance." He darted a look back at them, then toward the machine. "You can't stop me. I know this location. If you drag me away now, I'll merely come back later, when you aren't looking. You cannot have eyes on me all the time. This will take but a moment. Think of the benefits when we know how this works."

Surely he didn't think they would let him get away with this? Rilan looked to Origon, to Vethis, and back. She had to do something, quickly.

Origon locked eyes with her, pointed to her, to Vethis, and then tapped his temple. Rilan looked aghast at him. Was he saying what she thought? It was an intrusion of the worst kind.

Origon raised his bushy eyebrows and pointed to the man's back.

Rilan took a deep breath, stepping quietly across the floor, using training her father taught her in her youth to step silently. Vethis hadn't looked a second time, absorbed in the details of the hiss-tick machine, hands moving quickly over the controls. She heard the Symphony of his body come into clarity as she got closer, then the more subtle Symphony of his mind. She would need to touch him for this to work, but she gathered the pieces of the Symphony in her mind beforehand, noting where she would use her song to make adjustments to chemicals in his brain.

She hesitated only for a moment, standing behind him. He was still adjusting dials, directing the machine to give him the stolen abilities. Hers were not the heroic actions the Council championed, but she was still serving the people of the Great Assembly. She couldn't imagine a Nether with Vethis in control of three houses, any more than Ket, or anyone else, for that matter.

He must have finally heard or felt something, but he turned too late. Rilan put her open palm on his glossy black hair.

She changed his mind.

It was a complex adjustment, burning away memories of the last few days. Much of it she had to do quickly as she encountered the deeper levels of the Symphony defining his mind, catching notes and musical phrases as they flew past. Many sections went almost too fast, but she kept on, her lips pressing together. He fought back, weakly, but he was surprised and she had the full measure of his Symphony. She merely brushed his efforts away. This was her discipline. She was a psychologist. And she was a majus of the House of Healing.

She was supposed to help people with mental issues, not take advantage of them. It was so easy to slide into rationalizing that this was necessary. This would be the first and last time she did such a thing.

Rilan found his hatred of her along the way, burning as brightly as hers of him. She peeked at the chords, surprised to recognize jealousy and shame among them, even more than the hatred. She could just…

No. She resisted the urge to remove it, and gave that tiny win to her conscience. She understood a little better now why he antagonized her. But why was he jealous? If he just applied himself, he could be every bit as effective as she was in the House of Healing.

From now on, every time he looked at her, every time he spoke, she would remember she had the opportunity to change that view of her, and hadn't. She would be the better person.

When she was done, Vethis sank down into a sleep similar to the one Ket had been in. Before he killed her. She wanted him to answer to the Council for his actions, but that was impossible now. He would recall nothing of the past three days. That was more important even than bringing this to the Council.

Rilan found her hands shaking, and not with fatigue. She looked to Origon and something in her face must have told him what she was thinking.

"This was to be the right thing to do," he said. "And this is what being a majus truly is. Are you understanding, now, why I spend so much time on the homeworlds and away from the Nether?"

Rilan thought she did, just a bit. Things happened out here. Things with no right or wrong answer. The Council, for all its power, could not control everything. It was up to the individual majus to do that. But too many maji stayed in the Nether, preferring to turn a blind eye. His words sank in, and her next question became clear.

"With Ket dead, there's no proof here any longer." After the results of Vethis' betrayal, they must get rid of this threat forever. "Should we really give the research to the Council?"

Origon gave her a lopsided half-smile, several pointy teeth showing on one side. "What do you think they will be doing with the knowledge?"

Rilan thought for several moments on that, listening to the hiss-tick that filled the silent room. She eyed Vethis, curled up on the floor.

"Even if they kept it secret, sooner or later someone would come along with more ambition than sense."

"Someone like him?" Origon nodded at the slumbering Vethis.

Rilan grimaced at the thought of Vethis ever being on the Council. That would be the day.

"So what do we do with it?" She looked around the cavern.

"We destroy it," Origon answered, as if that had been his plan all along.

It took time, but they disconnected all the machinery from the pipes and from the steam generators. Rilan bent the ends of the pipes so they wouldn't connect to the machines again easily. Origon was the one to destroy the research. She thought he might make some grand change to the House of Power to cause them to combust, but instead he produced a set of matches from somewhere in his robe.

"Sometimes easier is to be better." He set the pile of notes alight.

Rilan watched the journals burn. "Someday I'll be on the Council. I'll make it so these things don't happen anymore."

Origon only smiled at her. "But first, I am hoping you'll travel with me. This has been…exciting."

Rilan thought over the last several days and shook her head. "Exciting" wouldn't have been her first choice of words.

"We should hide the cave entrance, too," she said.

Councilor Feldo was manning the portal ground at the Spire of the Maji when they came back to the Nether. Rilan knew even the councilors were not exempt from this duty, but she had never actually *seen* one at the post.

"Celebrating your success?" the councilor asked, arching an eyebrow at the limp form of Vethis slung between them. They had left Ket's body in the cave with her equipment, under a pile of rubble. Origon had been adept at exploiting hidden faults in the cave system with the House of Power. It was unlikely anyone would find it now. "I am surprised Apprentice Vethis accompanied you."

"Merely a short trip to be exploring the possibilities inherent in becoming a majus," Origon said.

"You did suggest we should work together," Rilan added, smiling innocently.

Councilor Feldo only grunted at them, his bushy black beard pointing accusingly until they left the portal ground.

They dropped Vethis off in his room. He would wake up thinking he had celebrated far too heavily the night before with his rich cronies. Rilan knew it wasn't an uncommon thing for him, and his friends likely wouldn't be able to remember either. Another few days lost to intoxicants.

They collapsed at Origon's apartment. They both needed to use his bath.

"I'll need to find another place to live, now that I'm a majus," Rilan told him.

"You were never giving me an answer, before," he said.

"Will I travel with you?"

Origon nodded.

Rilan found she didn't have to think as hard about that as she expected. "Will there be more like this?"

"Much more," he said, his crest fluttering in excitement.

"Then maybe next time we can find a proper inn or hostel to stay in while we travel," Rilan told him.

Origon gave her a full pointy smile—the one that disconcerted most of her species, but not her. "With a comfy bed."

Rilan smiled back. "I'll bring my things up tonight, then." She started to get up from one of his overstuffed chairs.

"I will be needing to contact Wint, to send my brother's body back," Origon said, getting up as well. "He is likely wondering where we went and hoping we also are not going to turn up dead in the forest."

"They do like to avoid hubbub," Rilan added, and was rewarded with a sad smile from Origon.

He went to the mantle, pulling one piece of paper from his pocket, and picking up a portrait. It was the same one she had seen before, of him and his brother, both looking much younger.

"What is that?" Rilan asked.

Origon looked guilty only for a moment. "A memento. I was going to be saving it to remind me of this."

Rilan crossed to him quickly and snatched the paper from him. Her eyes widened as she realized what it was.

"What are you doing?" she cried. The paper was one of Ket's journal entries, describing how the abilities of the majus of the House of Potential transferred to her. "If this became public, someone could replicate Ket's work. I didn't attack a colleague and erase his memory just for you to mess it up!"

Origon's jaw worked, but he said nothing. Gently, he put the picture back on the mantle. His hand went to his moustaches, running down their length. Slowly, Rilan looked around his apartment, filled with knick-knacks and trinkets from all over the ten homeworlds. What else was hidden here?

She thrust the paper back at him. "Burn it," she said. "Burn it, or you can have adventures by yourself."

Origon took the paper back, sighed, and nodded at her. "I like to keep…items to remind me of my travels. But you are to be correct. I am not thinking straight, still." He glanced to the picture, then back to her. "This is to be why I need you with me. I have been too long by myself, traveling among the homeworlds." He concentrated on the paper between his fingertips. An orange aura swept up it, followed by flame. The paper crumpled, but Origon watched her.

Rilan understood. The fire was not a reversible change. Origon would lose notes of his song by making it, but he wanted her to know he was serious.

"You will come with me now?" he asked.

"Yes," she answered.

"Then there is to be one more thing. You must call me 'Ori' from now on," he told her.

Well, it's shorter, Rilan thought. *It will be easier to get his attention, the next time we're fighting for our lives.*

"It was something only Delphorus called me," he continued. "I was never to be fond of it, but now I am thinking I will be wanting to hear the term again, to remind me of him. I am also thinking you would be the only one I could bear to call me that." He was looking down, at the paper crumbling to ash, but she could hear his voice shake.

Rilan couldn't speak for a moment, fighting around the lump in her throat. She wasn't an emotional woman.

"I would be honored, Ori," she said.

ACKNOWLEDGEMENTS

Many people helped this book become a reality. Thanks first to my wife, Heather, for putting up with many nights of ignoring her while I was writing. She gives me excellent feedback and is my favorite sounding board (as well as being a few of my other bests and favorites). Second, a big thank you to my alpha and beta readers: James Olinda, Drew Gula, Dave W, David Vizcaino, Courtney Brooks, Reese Hogan, and all the folks at Reading Excuses for critiquing my submissions. Robin Duncan gets a special shout-out for excellent critiques and suggestions through several stories set in this universe. Thanks to Shrike76 for the suggestion of using "song." Thanks to Micah Epstein for the awesome cover and interior art. Check out his paintings at micahepstein.blogspot.com. Finally, many thanks to the members of the Writing Excuses podcast for spending their valuable time teaching and encouraging new writers. Without their advice, this would likely have never been published.

ABOUT THE AUTHOR

I am a North Carolina native and a lifelong fan of science fiction and fantasy. In no particular order, I am a mechanical engineer, a karate instructor, a video and board gamer, a reader, and a writer. In my spare time, I wrangle three cats and somewhere between one and six guinea pigs, and my wife wrangles me (not an easy task). We both enjoy putting our pets in cute little costumes and then taking pictures of them repeatedly. You can visit my website at williamctracy.com.

If you liked what you saw of Rilan, Origon, and the Dissolutionverse, look for more stories coming in the near future. If you didn't like Rilan or Origon, there will be other stories that do not feature them. The universe is a big place. And if you are wondering why it is called the Dissolutionverse, stay tuned…

Please take a moment to review this book at your favorite retailer's website, or Goodreads, or simply tell your friends! I appreciate all honest feedback.

Thanks for reading!
William C Tracy